HIGH WATER

HIGH WATER

by

Richard Bissell

An Atlantic Monthly Press Book

Little, Brown and Company · Boston · Toronto

ATLANTIC-LITTLE, BROWN BOOKS
ARE PUBLISHED BY
LITTLE, BROWN AND COMPANY
IN ASSOCIATION WITH
THE ATLANTIC MONTHLY PRESS

Published simultaneously in Canada
by Little, Brown & Company (Canada) Limited

PRINTED IN THE UNITED STATES OF AMERICA

For Medio

A river, a very big and powerful river, is the only natural force that can wholly determine the course of human peregrination.

T. S. ELIOT

HIGH WATER

*Captain, why don't you hire some real roust-
abouts from Calloway County, them levee rats
from St. Louis ain't no good.*

—STEAMBOAT BILL HECKMAN

1

THE Grease Cup was right there in front of Katz's
drugstore, waiting for me like he said he would be.

"Hello, Grease Cup," I said. "It looks like you got the worst
of it."

"What a night," he said.

"Old lady not so good?"

"Just the same," he said. "Where was you at?"

"Me and Lucille got a room at the hotel."

"Who's Lucille?"

"She's the one with her picture stuck in my mirror."

"Oh. Yeah. That brunette with all the hair."

"Let's get a cab," I said.

"I ain't got but two dollars. Let's walk."

The Grease Cup looked unhappy, in his blue serge suit, maroon shirt and tie to match, unhappy as he always did after a half an hour ashore. He was a big man, with a round flushed face, and his especial pride and joy was a gray felt hat for which he had paid nine dollars one night in Peoria when we were stuck in the ice below town. But the hat was a half size too small, which made him look like a greenhorn from Nebraska.

"Old lady worked you mighty clean," I said. "What does she think you're gonna buy beer and cigarettes with between here and St. Paul and back?"

"She thinks I set in the engine room all that time. But I always keep twenty, thirty dollars on the boat."

"Let's get a cab," I said.

"O.K., if you pay for it," he said, shifting his black shiny fiberboard suitcase from one hand to the other.

"How come the suitcase?" I said. "Come on," I said. "There's a cab stand down the street."

"Old lady consented to iron a few shirts for me by some miracle or other."

We got into a cab and I told the driver to take us to the Northern Transit Barge Line docks, but he never heard of it so I told him where to go.

"Well, here we are again," the Grease Cup said. "Thank God." And the sun came out from behind a cloud and lit with great effect through the sky-view top on his big front gold tooth.

It was early in April and the sky was filled with scudding clouds. Whenever one passed in front of the sun all of St. Louis suddenly looked dismal, cold, and dirty. Then again the sun would come out and it was warm and almost baseball time. But the times when the sun was under were more than when it was out, and that's the way St. Louis is, it looks worse more often than it looks good.

"I don't suppose you heard no orders," the Grease Cup said.

"I called in. They're giving us eight loads."

"Eight! My God don't them fools know there's a flood coming down at us."

"They figure we'll get through," I said. "I spose they wanna show River Transit and Marine Barge what big operators we are."

"I don't envy you none as Mate. Why we'll be double-tripping and likely as not smacking bridges all the way."

"Casey and Ironhat won't hit no bridges," I said. "Casey and Ironhat won't hit nothing."

"I can think up better pilots than them two. I wisht old man Livingston was aboard."

"Well he's dead so what's the use talking about Livingston?"

"I can think up better pilots than them two wise guys."

"Quit talking like an engineer," I said. "Listen, Casey's *good,* don't forget it, and Ironhat's careful. If Ironhat don't wanna run no bridges why Casey will run 'em for him. Casey could take the *Muscatine* through the Hennepin Canal and never touch the banks."

"That would be an interesting sight, seeing she's a hunnred feet longer than the locks."

"Leave it to Casey," I said.

The sun was under again and we were going down back streets and past vacant lots and beat-up apartment houses with stained-glass front doors that must have been the class about fifty years ago, but now they had tin cans on the sidewalk and colored kids on the curbstones, and pieces of the stained glass were busted or missing.

"I hope Clarence took aboard plenty groceries. This looks like a long trip to me," the Grease Cup said.

"I thought you liked them long trips. I thought the only reason you come steamboatin was to get away from the old lady. Ain't you never satisfied?"

"Eight loads is four too many on a stage of river like this."

"Where'd you go last night, anyplace?"

"She wanted to go to the goddam show. Jimmy Stewart. She thinks he's just the cutest boy around. I says, 'Honey let's go to some nice quiet little old night club and see the floor show.'"

"So you went to the movies."

"Yeah, we went to the movies."

"I didn't go to no movie."

"You ain't got the old lady, neither."

"Why in hell don't you unload that old lady? You got no kids. She's just nothin but misery. Danged if I'd put up with that."

"I ain't sure if this is the right way," the cab driver said. "Is this right?"

"Yeah, you're O.K.," I said. "Turn right two blocks up here at the warehouse."

The sun was under again. Tell the truth, I didn't feel much like going back to the boat, but then, I never did and probably never will, even if I was to stay another fifty years on the river. Once I get my feet aboard and my store clothes off and I get the smell of the boat and the river, why I'm happy. But when I'm uptown in a clean shirt I never want to go back, I have to fight to make myself do it.

"That would hurt her feelings," the Grease Cup said, "if I was to leave her."

"Grease Cup," I said. "You are completely nuts."

"Where do I go now?" says the cab driver.

"Keep on straight," I said.

"Maybe the old lady would brighten up a little," I said, "if you moved to a small town upriver someplace. You know, like Hannibal, say, or Muscatine."

"Oh my God, no," he said. "She has to go to them big movie palaces with all the gilt and mirrors in the lobby or she'd be even worse. Why, say, she never missed a picture yet at any of the big movie houses downtown. Brother, she catches them *all*."

"You know something rather interesting, Grease Cup?" I said.

"What's that?" he said, looking out the window at some old board fences and an empty lot full of dry, dead weeds and rusty tin cans.

"I ain't married," I said.

"Ain't you marvelous," he said.

"Here we are," I said. "Leave us off right here by this gate. We'll walk from here."

"You fellas goin up the river on a boat?" the driver said as I was paying him off.

"That's right."

"Pretty high water ain't it?"

"That's what they say," I said.

"Well I wish you luck," he said.

"I hope we don't need none," the Grease Cup said, and we started through the debris that littered the yard in front of the office. There were oil drums and coils of old cable, junk line tied up in bales to be sold, an antique marine engine with the head off and the cylinders filled with rain water, and unidentifiable shapes of marine junk, rusty and forgotten, filling the area from the woven wire fence over to the office, a dirty frame building with bright green patches on the uneven roof.

We threaded our way down the path through the remnants and came upon a propeller, six feet in diameter, with one fluke bent over, split, and chewed to ragged pieces.

"There's a fine piece of Casey's work," the Grease Cup said, as he always did. "There's your great Casey for you."

"Quit talking like an engineer," I said. "Ain't no pilot living that never hit *something*."

"Old man Livingston ran Maquoketa Chute for fifty years and never found no bottom. But Casey, *he* managed to find a rock as big as the Court House. How he done it nobody knows except him. That's his special pilotin secret. Most pilots couldn't of found that rock with a soundin pole. He not only found it, he run the boat on it to prove it."

"You got Casey on the brain. Whyn't you go home to that old lady and give it up? Whyn't you just plain give the river up, it bothers you so."

"It don't bother me that much," he said.

"You could get a stationary engineer's job at the Waterworks and never miss a double-feature show."

"I'm goin aboard," he said, "and see what's cookin."

I went into the office to see if I had any mail. I had a letter from a girl in Winona, Minnesota, named Alma. Her old man was an engineer on the Winona, Green Bay, and Northern, but it didn't make her any more interesting. She was only just good for one thing. Then I had my magazines: *Hunter, Trader and Trapper, Waterways Journal,* and *Railroad.* And another lesson from that correspondence course, which increased my St. Louis blues by reminding me that I was already a lesson behind on account of the layover. I never can get anything done with my head anyplace except on a steamboat. That's why I was better off on the river: no whiskey, no dolls, no ball games and shows and taverns. It's no temptation when you can't get at such things. Nothing but the boat and twelve hours' watch every day and no distractions on every corner with electric signs over them saying BUDWEISER.

Cap Wilson, the Port Captain, came out of his office. He was a little bald-headed fat guy, a crack pilot when he was on the boats, now suffering from the joys of promotion and shore life.

"I hear we got eight," I said.

"What about it?" he said.

"Pretty high water," I said.

"Leave that to Casey and Ironhat," he said.

"That's just what I'm about to do," I said.

I walked down to the boat, and the sun went under for good. I stood and looked at the Mississippi. She was high and she looked ugly as hell. I looked up at the sky and it was all overcast by now, and a breeze was coming up from the northeast that smelled like more rain. With the sun under it was chilly and miserable and I went aboard.

I walked down the guard and past the engine room where I saw the Grease Cup standing in there talking to the oiler; he looked mighty funny in his store clothes and Nebraska Saturday-night hat. The oiler was wiping his hands on some waste and giving the Cup some big story to explain all the things he had forgot to do since the Second had gone up to the nearby tavern for a drink.

I climbed up the stairs and opened the door to my room, right behind the compressed air tanks lying aft of the pilothouse on the boiler deck. Inside it smelled mighty poor. Jackoniski, the bastard, was laying there reading *Amazing Detective* and punching his cigarettes out in a sawed-off Pet milk can, and never a window open in the world, or the door either.

"Well you goddam imported Polish ham," I said. "Why in the hell ain't you out on deck and if not when did they pass this law again opening a window? This place smells worse than a deck hand's glove."

Jackoniski was an easygoing, stupid dog like most of the boys I ever had to share a bunkroom with. He shaved every other day and of all the Second Mates in the company they could have dumped on me he was the world's worst. If you stood right behind Jackoniski with a club he would make a good Mate; he had been on the barge lines long enough and he knew the work. But he always wanted to go sit down someplace and he didn't give a damn if the deck hands spent twenty minutes over their 10 A.M. coffee.

"They ain't nothin goin on," he said, "so I decide to come up and lay down awhile."

"Well it stinks in here with you and your cigarettes," I said. "And for Christ sake, get your socks out of the washbowl. Here," I said, and tossed his Rockford sox, damp, onto his face.

"You been away so long," he said, "I almost forgot you was so sweet."

I took off my clothes without saying anything more, hung my pants and jacket over a wire hanger with my shirt inside under the jacket, wrapped my shoes in a newspaper and stuck them under the bunk, and put on my tan pants and my shirt that had NORTHERN TRANSIT embroidered on the back (and N.T. on the pocket).

"I spose you know we got eight," I said.

"Yeah," he said. "So what?"

"So nothing," I said. "Except this trip as long as I'm Mate and you're Watchman by God if we run into trouble you ain't agoin to be layin in that bunk very long." "Watchman" is what they call Second Mate on the Mississippi.

"I take my orders from Casey," he said.

Just to be a bastard he threw his cigarette over his shoulder into the washbasin. Nothing I hate like a cigarette butt in the washbowl when I go to brush my teeth or something. That's your Jackoniski for you.

I went down to the galley and got a cup of coffee. The minute I saw Clarence in his white pants and undershirt I lost those old St. Louis blues and forgot all about Lucille and room 924, and the dirty alleys, and the zoo, and the high water and the eight loads, I felt like the boy coming home. Now this was something I knew all about, nothing that could ever happen on this boat would ever surprise or scare me, but uptown, well, there are so damn many things going on that a person just simply can't understand.

"Hello, Duke," says Clarence in that friendly way he's got, like he was so happy to see you back. "Boy am I glad to see you back!"

"Don't I always come back?" I said.

"Mostly," he said. "Except Peoria, and Helena, and Dubuque, and Wood River, and . . ."

"Never mind," I said. "I always come back. Them times was merely miscalculations."

"There is a fresh pot over there," he said. "I do believe this trip is going to be interesting to say the lease."

"You can repeat that," I said. "Are Casey and Ironhat aboard?"

"Casey is laying down," he said, creasing four pie crusts. "Ironhat went over to the saloon for a box of cigars."

The coffee was good and the galley was the best place on earth, and I stood there looking out the door across the guard at the current; she was really going on past like she meant it, with a lot of bubbles and twigs and scum.

"That's a mean-looking river," I said.

"When ain't it mean?" he said.

I went to the range and refilled.

"Well, we only got two from here over Chain of Rocks, anyways," he said, opening the oven door.

Whatever was up the river, I thought—standing there in my nice clean pants and shirt, with the cap on my head with two stars on it—whatever was upriver I could at least understand it; I felt at least I could always meet the Mississippi River on equal terms, as they say.

"I been fighting with her for thirteen years," I said. "I don't honestly believe, Clarence, that she has any more surprises for me."

A towboat from out of the Missouri River, the *Far West*, came sliding past with four empties, quiet and slick and going like a bat out of hell.

"Look," says Clarence. "Look at *Far West* go. Man, look at that current take her down."

"What kinda pies are them in the oven?" I said.

"Logumberry," he said.

"I never heard of such a thing," I said.

"You'll eat it just the same," he said.

The *Far West* went down-river so fast I had to lean out the galley door to see her any more and as I leaned out a drop of rain hit me on the wrist.

"Here comes that rain," I said.

"Blowing from the east, ain't it?" Clarence said, coming to the door and standing beside me with a cup of coffee.

"Yeah," I said. "Two days of rain and this here trip north is gonna get interesting."

"Don't tell me the river has got you worried too? I never thought she would ever get you down, Duke"—it was Casey.

His Master's Voice. I turned back into the galley, letting the door slam behind me on the Mississippi River, already almost in flood stage, with the raindrops pattering onto its gliding surface.

"Hello, Casey," I said. "When are we gonna turn loose and head north?"

Anyway I was all over it, as I always am, by the time we had the logumberry pies for dinner at 5:45 P.M., right in the middle of the Chain of Rocks, which is a bad place right above St. Louis with rock bottom and very bad currents every which way. Even with only two barges strung out two long ahead, why we certainly didn't set any speed records going up through there that afternoon in the drizzle and mist.

"Who in the hell ever heard of a logumberry pie?" Ironhat said, going into his second piece.

Clarence leaned in the doorway to the galley and smoked a cigarette in a cigarette holder he had won on a punchboard deal.

"Well you heard of it now," he said. "I reckon your stomach don't care too much what it's called."

At the far end of the table two deck hands got up silently and went out. The wiper, low man of the engine department, sat dunking sugar cookies into his coffee. Every once in a while he would lose a piece and fish it out of his coffee with a spoon. It was driving Ironhat nuts, I could see. But Ironhat never said anything in a critical way to anybody, except maybe excited he would holler at the deck hands out of the pilothouse, but in a way so they didn't get sore at him.

However . . . "Is it absolutely necessary you got to slop around in that coffee cup with them cookies?" says the Second Engineer, a new man last trip. He had stomach ulcers and you could see him in the engine room at night, making himself a shot of baking soda in a special glass, amidst the terrible noise and uproar of the diesels. His name was Kennedy and he wasn't very happy.

The wiper looked embarrassed and went out, pulling his black sateen cap out of his hip pocket en route.

"Goddam fine boat where we have to eat at the same

table with the wipers and the deck hands. Too bad we ain't fattening up a hog and we could have him at table too."

Clarence didn't care much for this remark and he said, "The officers eat by themselves on the Federal Barge Line. Now if you had steam license you could go over there and you wouldn't have to eat with the riffraff."

Of course the Second Engineer had no steam license in the world, all he knew was injectors and the Briggs oil filter and such things, so he got up mad and went out.

"I love these big shots," Clarence said.

"Now he will have to hit the baking soda harder than ever this watch," Ironhat said. "Why do you insist on riling him up that way, Clarence?"

"If Kennedy don't like it here why don't he move on?" Clarence said. "Damn if I would work on a job where I had to guzzle a half-pound Arm and Hammer every watch."

Everything in the messroom rattled and shook and the salt cellars and the patent sugar dispenser with the hinged spout jumped up and down on the worn white tablecloth as the boat passed over some shoal water.

"Jesus keep it in the deep water, Casey," says Clarence the cook, "or we won't have no dishes left."

"Boy she sure gives you a swell shaking up in the shallow water," I said. "I don't believe they designed this here hull according to Hoyle. The way she chatters in shoal water beats anything I ever seen."

"This would be a fine night to be walking up the sidewalk someplace in central Illinois," Ironhat said, putting the cellophane off a new cigar into the remains of his logumberry pie and striking a wood match on the underside of the table.

"We are not setting no speed records going up through here," said Deck hand number 3 still down at the end of the table, forking his pie and entering into his third cup of coffee.

"We ain't likely to set no records," Ironhat said.

"I sure don't like this steamboatin on a near flood," Clarence says.

"That makes two of us," Ironhat said.

We were now parted by some boatmen, and
were so exorsted that it was more than a month
before either of us could fight.

—DAVY CROCKETT

2

BACK home in Minnesota about the time that Rod
La Rocque was playing at the Princess with Jobyna Ralston
in *Gigolo,* and maybe even now for all I know, there was
always a two-line notice someplace in the back of the paper
under the column headed LOCALS, which said:

Expert Truss Fitters
KASSMEYER'S DRUGSTORE

Across the page was a comic strip called Salesman Sam.
Sam worked for a boss called Guzzelem who ended up every
few days swallowing his cigar in the last box of the strip.

There was sometimes a dead fish on the counter of the store labeled 5¢.

Anyway, my old man was the expert truss fitter advertised every night in the paper, and in addition he waited on trade, in a neatly pressed gray coat, and sold paper-wrapped bottles of Dr. Caldwell's Senna Laxative and Dr. Schiffman's Asthmador Cigarettes (with instructions on "how to inhale") and Lithiated Buchu (drives out foreign matter in the kidneys and decreases excessive acid, thereby relieving irritation), and it was always Pop who got the unhappy boys and girls who came in and stammered out a request for certain embarrassing products. In between times my father, who looked a little bit like this lanky old John Carradine in the movies, only not so positive, would slip behind the sticky soda fountain to squirt out cherry Cokes and chocolate marshmallow sundaes and Supreme Double Dip Delights with Mixed Nuts for the after-movie crowd, and when business was slow around 3:30 P.M. he would get a broom from behind the door into the truss room, which was back behind the pharmacy room, and sweep the sidewalk. Then on Thursday nights he trimmed the windows, removing last week's pyramid of dummy Ipana boxes, and setting up a new display, maybe of Noxzema or Williams Shaving Cream. For all these efforts to please, Mr. Kassmeyer paid my father $32.50 a week and that was as far as he was ever going to go, and we all knew it, as Kassmeyer had a son in grade school (who took violin lessons) who would take over about the time Kassmeyer was ready to go home permanently and sit out the long Minnesota summer afternoons on the porch with a palm-leaf fan imprinted with local advertising in his hand.

With bacon at 16 cents a pound and a pair of good tough shoes for a growing boy priced at $2.65 down at the Popular Clothing and Furnishings Store this stupendous salary of my poor old Pa's was enough to get by on and have a roast on

the table once a week and me not feel queer at school because the other kids had something or other I didn't have.

> *The trees stood like sentinels*
> *And the nighthawks dove*
> *Endlessly above the*
> *Evening rooftops.*
> *Purple-gray, the bluffs*
> *Of mighty Mississippi,*
> *(Endlessly flowing into*
> *the mystery beyond)*
> *Rise . . .*

That's the kind of poetry my girl friend Roma Schlesinger
used to write for the high school paper; her father was a poor
old disappointed professor of English at Mount Union College there in Wacoutah City. They printed this poem in the
front of the high school yearbook and everybody thought
it was pretty artistic.

Poor old Professor Schlesinger. There must be a lot of him
around at these county-seat colleges. One trouble with
Schlesinger was he had been to Harvard for some course in
Shakespeare or something, so he had two strikes against him
even if he hadn't of been a professor. These small-town jokers
who sign their name with an X can have more fun over Harvard or Yale or one of them Eastern colleges than they can
kidding the wife about her new hat. Especially Harvard.

One of the most rugged affairs I can remember was one
time Roma finally prevailed on the old folks to let her have a
party. The professor had one thing he thought more of than
Shakespeare even, and that was this walnut table he had
got when he was down there at Harvard; the story was that
Shakespeare himself or Longfellow or somebody had used to
write on it. Well there is nothing like one of these parties
when you were in the ninth grade, with the girls on one side
of the room and the boys on the other shoving each other,

which went on for about an hour before the Winkum game started. So during the shoving period Fat Mason shoved Johnny Kaiser onto the famous table and it went down for the count. About all it was good for after that was stove wood.

That was Professor Schlesinger, a nice old guy to tell the truth, who had long since given up trying to find anybody who either wanted to talk about Shakespeare or give him credit for talking about it either. I'll bet my old man, when you come down to the financial end of it, made more money per week at the drugstore than Professor Schlesinger. Not that Mount Union College didn't pay more than $32.50 a week to a professor, theoretically, but it was merely they never had any money in the cash register on Friday night, so Roma's Daddy he never knew from one week to the next whether he could pay off the corner grocery store or not.

I remember also we had a theory in those days when a house burned down it was usually caused by "a mouse nibbled some matches."

I came home full of it one night and Pop was sitting in the kitchen played out from a tough day with difficult truss problems. He was sitting there reading the *Times-Journal* and Ma was filling up his coffee cup again.

"Gee, Pop," I said, "this house over on Dakota Street burnt clear to the ground. Boy was it ever a keen fire. Me and Charlie Schroeder saw the whole thing."

"You better go up to bed," Ma said.

"I suppose you mean 'Charlie Schroeder and I,' not 'me and Charlie Schroeder.' Whose house was it?" Pop said, turning the *Times-Journal* inside out and beating it over his leg.

"I don't know, boy it was some terrible fire. There was three engines there, number five, number two, and number one."

"How did the fire start?" Pop said.

"A mouse nibbled some matches," I said.

"That so?" Pop said. "Who saw him?"

"Who saw who?" I said.

"The mouse," Pop said.

I went up to bed to think it over and have been thinking it over ever since.

Next day I went to school and there was the usual mob shoving around the door after old lady McNulty came out with the bell and rung it, with the usual morning conversation such as:

"Quit yer shovin, Hadley."

"I ain't shovin it's McNeely."

"Look out Hantleman if you ain't lookin for a good poke."

"Is that so? Who says so?"

"Quit yer shovin, Mardaus."

"I ain't shovin."

"You'll get somethin you ain't lookin for if you don't look out, Reider."

"Yeah, who says so?"

"Come on, Hadley, cut the comedy."

"Somebody around here's gonna get something they ain't lookin for."

Etc., etc. This is about all the conversation I can remember from grade school. So anyway I got my pal Fats Murdock aside and I said, "Say that was a swell fire, huh?"

"Yeah, boy! Swell."

"Listen," I said. "Who seen the mouse nibble on the matches?"

"Heck, I don't know," Fats says, "but you can see for yourself that's what happened."

"I don't see nothing of the kind," I said. "What's so blame positive about it? Where is the mouse at now?"

"Oh you make me sick," he says. "That's the way it *was*

that's all. Why most all your fires start that way, ask anybody."

But I quit school, right in the middle of *Allen and Greenough's Latin Grammar,* and set out to see the world. All due to reading too many adventure stories in the senior high school library, combined with a spring day outside that was driving the whole Middle West crazy. I bummed out to Chamberlain, South Dakota, and looked at the Missouri River for a while, and I bummed out to the Rockies and looked at them, and I got rained on in Seattle and insulted in Skagway and kicked by a horse outside of Cody, and beat up in Bakersfield and loved to death in New Orleans—I was some hot shot I was. Finally drifted back, like all natural-born bums, to the old home territory. Wandered around, worked on the section, gave the girls quite a bit of sweet talk, ended up in Quincy, Illinois, mighty low and took a job going decking on a steamboat.

Oh my yes I had a very glamorous impression of myself when I would walk down the street in Cheyenne, Wyoming, far from Kassmeyer's Drugstore and far from Roma Schlesinger. I was hot stuff out West; hell I went to San Francisco and saw the ships come in from way out in the Pacific Ocean through the Golden Gate and slept around in flophouses and in culverts and boxcars and ditches and on ratty old mattresses and in the Y.M.C.A. and in those $1.50 hotels with a pitcher of ice water and an extra blanket one-sixteenth-inch thick in the second drawer of the dresser. I have been in all the hobo camps out there in the great West along the Santa Fe right of way and been hustled to the edge of town and told to Move On We Don't Need No More Bums Here in This Town. I've seen the sun set on all the Coca Cola signs west of Dodge City; hell I've been to the Indian pow-wows where the tourists stand around and buy post cards and I've been out there in the Arizona deserts where the saguaro cactus grows fifty feet high. I've been in Fort Dodge, Iowa, and in Paducah and in Calumet, Michigan, where the Calumet and Hecla has all their big buildings. Yes and I've been over to Van Wert, Ohio, in a snowstorm when traffic was tied up for two days, and bummed the freights from Galesburg, Illinois, all the way to the slums of Los Angeles—all through the West—been to Gillette, Wyoming, and got into a barroom fight, had the hell kicked out of me in an old midnight saloon east of Spokane a few miles, but mostly nowadays that I am settled down and have clean sheets to sleep between and an all-wool blanket, the thing I can remember is walking down the railroad track around sundown beside a freight train someplace out in Colorado. I can hear the brakeman walking down on the other side of the cars with his feet crunching in the cinders on some special hot old night near the Rocky Mountains. I can't remember the name of the town but I remember the evening—that's the evening when I thought everything was going to be swell and I would marry some girl with a fifty-thousand-dollar smile and have steak for breakfast and six healthy kids who would soon put me on a pension and just come around on Sunday afternoons to let me see the new baby.

That's the place I want to go back to someday—Colorado—what a state that is, there's the golden goddam West for you.

Then I came back to the river valley for a while again. I went up home to Wacoutah City to see the folks and check up on the progress in the truss-fitting dept., the Noxzema, foot powder, and false-teeth stickum game. It was seven years since I had run off and lo and behold both my folks was dead, burned up in our old house there on East River Street.

"How did the fire come about? How did it happen?" I says. "I suppose a mouse ate some matches."

"No," says old man Kassmeyer. "They say it was faulty wiring in the basement."

"What happened to Roma Schlesinger?" I said.

"They moved out of town," Kassmeyer says. "The professor is teaching in some little college in North Dakota."

"How could he find a college littler than Mount Union?" I said.

Well the hell with all this home-town stuff—I went and collected the old man's $1000 insurance and left town and never have I set foot there again or ever care to unless I need a truss sometime, as Kassmeyer has taken over where Pop left off, so he told me, and he was one of the best fitters in the game.

It is kind of funny when you figure all the various adventures I had that I would end up here Mate on a towboat, shoving a bunch of coal barges from St. Louis to the towns along the Upper Mississippi that nobody ever heard of like Dubuque, Cassville, Lansing, Genoa, Lake City and Red Wing, but there is something about it which you might call Romance, or you might call it feeble-mindedness depending on your age and state of mind, which gets under your skin and you can't seem to get away from it; somehow there is one hell of a lot of charm, as the travel folders say, about the Upper Mississippi River especially if you see it from the river and not from Highway 61 where you are trying to get to St. Paul in time to get a room and change to a clean shirt in time for the floor show up the street.

I can say "the hell with all this home-town stuff," but that is too easy. A person can't dispose of the home-town stuff so nice and simple as all that there is a great deal more to it. Where did the hanging lamp with all the colored glass in it go to, for example, that hung over our dining-room table all those years? You mean to say that glass lampshade, the first thing I remember on earth, is gone just because the house burnt up with my folks in it? And who seen the mouse?

I haven't even got a first, second, or third cousin, uncle, aunt, or nothing. Well I don't care about it much only I never wrote the folks; figured I would come home all fattened up and with a bronzed weather-beaten look, soldier of fortune, high cheekbones, squinty eyes from the Western sun and such, and drawling like Gary Cooper—but it didn't work out. They were both burnt up when I got there.

"You should of kept in touch with them," the Grease Cup used to say. "What could you expect? That's life, boy."

Many the hot night I used to walk out on the barges when we were off watch, and sit down with the Grease Cup or One Eye or somebody and listen to the river gurgling against the head of the tow as we shoved upstream, and talk or just sit and watch the hills or the little towns go by. But once in a while I would talk about this subject of my folks.

"Forget it," the Grease Cup would say. "There ain't nothin to be done about it now anyways."

All the same I used to bring it up once in a while. It always made me feel better about the entire affair to tell the Grease Cup about it and hear him say "Forget it. Nothing to be done about it anyways."

So I fought it out on deck and got to be Mate and that's all I want, I don't care to advance another inch up the ladder of Success on the river. I see these pilots sweating out their twelve hours per day and No Thanks, that river is too long, too big, too filled with junk waiting to be hit for this old boy. I wouldn't make a pilot anyway I am too goddam nervous I would die over 1000 deaths every watch. If it is all the same to everybody I will just continue on as Mate where I know what to do and when; and where I haven't got the responsibility for a $300,000 towboat, a string of barges worth $100,000, and the lives of twenty men. No thanks. I'll just sit here on the capstan and let the pilots worry while I merely light a Murad and act debonair.

Like Ironhat for example, he was the nervous type—he would spend six hours piloting in the pilothouse then go off watch and pilot six hours in his bunk. Now a Mate can relax when he goes off watch to some extent, providing of course he don't have some snake like this Jackoniski on his hands, which was the only trouble I had in the world on this job. Jackoniski was killing the romance of life on the Upper Mississippi to a large extent; a dog like that can spoil a spring day just by standing there breathing.

Yay, Blacksnake Baker, what's the matter of your boys this mornin'? Don't you still feel lucky when yer shed of redeye?

—JERKLINE

3

THAT'S enough about me for now, and all my problems and old-time history. Before I got off on that we were aboard the old *Royal Prince,* which is some name for an old diesel towboat, heading up toward Chain of Rocks above St. Louis.

We got up over the Chain of Rocks all right and Casey picked up a weather report on the short wave that said rain tonight and tomorrow in the St. Louis to Quincy area would be general. Casey was about to turn her off when the announcer says: "The continued rains in Minnesota and Wisconsin are causing floods along the Wisconsin River and in the Twin Cities area. Rain is still falling in these sections caus-

ing disruption of traffic due to road and bridge washouts."
Casey turned it off.

"That's fine," he said. "By the time we get to Dubuque the
locks will be out of commission and we'll have more water
than old Noah had, all piling right down on top of the mighty
motor vessel *Royal Prince*. Lovely, lovely. Very fine. Well,
Duke, I hope you have plenty line aboard."

"I got a whole new coil I been holding back," I said.

"That's good," he said. "I got a notion we'll need it."

I went down to get some cigarettes and Jackoniski was in
bed as usual reading a comic book. I told him to have his
boys sooge the galley after midnight and I went up to see
Grease Cup.

Then I was standing by the engine-room door. We were
passing Wood River and in the rain the Grease Cup and I
could see the deck hands on the *Marie O'Brien* going out to
turn her loose after loading with oil and just then in the
dusk a streak of lightning went down the sky and lighted up
everything you could see the leaves on the cottonwood trees
all silver on the underside where the wind was blowing
through and turning them over.

"Jesus Christ look at the water going down the shore," the
Grease Cup said, coming out of the engine room and leaning
against the unpainted door jamb. The setting sun was shining from over in Missouri through the light rain and over
the Illinois hills above the tall riverside trees the sky was
dark, dark blue and looking like Monday night in hell.

"You guys for the sweet Jesus I never heard nothing to
beat it you would think you never seen no water before,"
said Jackoniski working over his sharp white teeth with a
toothpick as he went past us in his underwear on the way
to the galley for a cup of coffee. "You boys just tickle the
hell out of me the way you go on about this here stage of
water."

"Don't forget to check the running lights on the tow to-night," I said. I never could count on him to remember the simplest things.

The rain began to fall a little harder and behind us now we could see the *Marie O'Brien* getting her head off the bank, and the deck hands coiling down the head lines they had pulled in off the bank. Well, you couldn't see what they were doing at that distance and through the rain, but you knew that's what they were doing and then after that you knew they would go back to the boat, stopping to check the couplings in a half-ass way, and then they would set around in the messroom for a while reading the new comic books the messboy had brought aboard, and smoke, and throw their gloves on the deck, and cuss the rain until they got up around the bend to Alton and had to get out on deck again and make the lock, standing there in the rain and looking up at the lockmen in the dark early evening under the electric lights.

The Grease Cup said nothing, but looked the other way. He wouldn't talk much to Jackoniski. He always said Jack-oniski shouldn't be on the boat at all. "He will probly turn out to be some famous pilot one of these days," he said. "Frankly," he said, "I wouldn't have him in the engine room more than one watch with me, and the sooner he moves on the better."

The sun set and the whole valley took on a funny nasty mustard color, very queer and unnatural. The wind was rising and kicking up a chop in the river as it met the down-bound current.

"Look at the drift," said the Grease Cup. "The Illinois must be running out already."

"Look at that damn queer color to everything," I said. "What's coming next, a tornado?"

Then that east wind blew the clouds over the last of the

sunset over in Missouri and night clapped down like somebody had throwed an old wet army blanket over the world.

"How late was you up last night?" the Grease Cup said.
"For my part I am gonna do some fancy sleepin at midnight."

"I would just as soon be at one of them double-feature
movies with your old lady now," I said.

"No you wouldn't," he said. "You like it out here. You're
crazy about it. You're a big Mate."

"That's right," I said. "They don't come any bigger. How's
them engines of yours for an argument with a flood?"

"They're all right. It's the steering I'm worried about.
There's something screwy with the relays and stuff and what
I know about electricity you could print on a buffalo nickel."

"That's fine," I said. "That will be as funny as a two-reel
comedy by Charles Chase if we lose our steering up in one
of these drawbridges with about six-mile-an-hour current."

"I ain't seen a Chase comedy in years," says the Grease
Cup. "I wonder what ever become of him. My but he was a
cut-up though."

It was as black out on deck as the inside of a Holstein
heifer. I went into the deck hands' bunkroom. Zero was lying
in the sack, squinting at a Donald Duck comic.

"When we get to St. Paul I'm gonna buy you an Uncle Wig-
gly book," I said. "He'd be just your speed."

"Who duh hell is Uncle Wiggler?" he said.

"Didn't you never hear of the kindly old rabbit gentleman?
Hell, he's a whizz. Right up your alley with Donald Duck
and Mickey Mouse and all them other uplifting characters
you are always studying up on."

"Aw cut it out," he says.

"Listen, get the light off and start snoring," I said. "We
might have a bad night the way it looks."

"O.K. boss," he said. "This here Donald Duck ain't got
much plot to it anyways."

Sometimes after dark, especially in the high water, when you can feel the river all around you but you can't see it, well, it's not too goddam soothing to the nerves. At night is the time when deck hands fall overboard and drown, when the pilots find some rock to hit and tear the bottom out of her, when the wind seems to blow harder and the rain to rain wetter and worse, and the hills to disappear. At night is the time when the couplings break and a barge gets loose, when the galley stove decides to blow up, when the steering (god forbid) goes out. At night is the time on the steamboats when the shaft busts or she blows a cylinder head or runs through herself. It always seems like the trouble happens at night, and trouble at night always seems twice as bad as trouble in the daytime when a person can see what the hell is going on.

Up in the pilothouse Casey reached up for the whistle cord and blew for the Alton lock.

I went out of the deck hands' bunkroom and stood on the guard and looked over at the lights of town. The rain for freshening up a little and I thought Duke, Son of Truss-Fitter, what an adventurer you turned out to be, boy.

cigarette after another and picking his teeth with a pocket-knife.

The boys had the last barrel in the water and were pulling it back aft when the Kid showed up.

He came up behind me from the road behind the office and I didn't see him at first, I was watching One Eye and Stevie fooling around with the oil drums.

"I come over here to join the boat," he says. "Are you the Captain? They tole me come on over here and the boat would be in here at about eight o'clock. I come from down here at Alton. Can't say I care much for it although my brother has a Model-A Ford in nice shape he leaves me drive it once in a while when he is feeling good. Old man run off three years ago and we ain't seen nothing of him since. Been working uptown four or five places. Brother Tim bellhoppin over to the hotel. Maw she got a waitress job at the Elite, you probly been in there already I imagine. So I decide to see if I can get on one of the boats my buddy Joe he is messboy on the *Wheelock Whitney* and he swears by it says it can't be beat so here I am. I am suppose to go deck hand."

"That's fine," I says. "But you ain't told me nothing about yourself. Where did you come from?"

"I come from down here at Alton," he says, setting his suitcase down between the railroad tracks. "My buddy Joe he is on the *Whitney*, he is messboy over there and he sure likes that job he says it is the best job he ever had and he has been to St. Paul nine times last summer and is on his way up there right now. My brother, he works over to the hotel bellhoppin he told me I was crazy to go off on the boats but my buddy Joe he says Tim is crazy and steamboatin is the only thing. Joe says once you have been steamboatin you won't want to never do another blessed thing except more of it. Maw works over at the Elite only she is mad at Mr. Kloston who runs the place, he is a Greek, and she says she might get another job one of these days, she is thinking of goin to the battery factory or maybe to household work. There is quite a demand for household work, down here at Alton now. Anyway Maw says, 'Go on, Delbert,' she says, 'if you wanna go off steamboatin you go right ahead,' she says, 'and send us a post card picture from St. Paul.'"

"Did you say Delbert?" I says.

"That's my name," the Kid says. "I was named after my uncle Delbert who is in the Caterpillar plant up to Peoria, my mother's brother he is. One time I was up to Peoria and he took me to the moving pictures and bought me a pair of roller skates, but that was when I was just a kid."

"You ain't no antique right now," I says. "How in the hell old are you anyway, boy?"

I couldn't see him blush it was that dark, but he squirmed a bit and he says, "Seventeen." If he was two days older than fifteen I'll be kicked from here to Memphis and back.

"Well listen, Delbert," I says. "It sounds to me like you have got the steamboat fever mighty bad and I can sympathize with you because I had the same symptoms once upon a time, but listen, Kid, just between you and me that ain't no kind of a name to come aboard a steamboat with. Ain't you got a middle name?"

The deck hands were hoisting the last barrel aboard, One Eye on the winch and Stevie down below.

"Mathewson," he said, the shortest sentence I ever heard him say.

"That ain't a bit of help," I said. "Come on, Kid, crawl aboard and we'll get this tow made up and start up after your buddy Joe on the *Whitney* and I sure hope they ain't got eight loads of fine Illinois coal like we have."

"Why?" he said, picking up his suitcase.

"Never mind," I said. "Come on with me, Kid."

"My name is Delbert," he says.

"No it ain't," I said. "It's just plain Kid from now on. Easy to remember, ain't it?"

So I went aboard, with the Kid stumbling along down the bank behind me, and I turned him over to One Eye, to show him where his bunk was and what to do next and where the water tap was at, and the Steersman-Clerk, a real earnest boy from college whose daddy owned some stock in the company, like most Steersmen in the world, come down to the bunkroom where the Kid was standing bewildered in the dark with only the light from a 40-watt bulb in the passage slanting into one end of the room, and got him to come out into the messroom, before he even had his good clothes off, and got him to answer over 1000 individual questions such as, When was you born and Where and Was your parents both Natives and if so, Why, and In case of a sudden death who should be notified and Who will pay Express Charges on the body, and Where did you work at last and Do you have any distinguishing bodily scars, marks, or interesting tattoos?

I meanwhile buzzed up the iron stairs to the pilothouse where Casey was sitting there with his gray felt hat shoved back, not looking anything like a river-boat pilot such as one might read about in the more popular magazines. He was talking over the short-wave radio to some boat up the Illinois River. I sat down and smoked a cigarette.

When he got through he went over to the starboard side and looked down at the bank where the boys had begun to carry the groceries aboard under the deck lights. I'm not the type Mate any more who gets down there and carries more stuff aboard than anybody else just as an example. I'm way past that stage and I don't mean Maybe. Especially since I got One Eye, who could mate the biggest tows in the whole inland waters only he simply don't care to, he prefers to be a deck hand, to keep an eye on things for me.

"Well," Casey says, "the trip don't look so very promising, Duke. In fact I doubt whether we'll get by without a lot of double-tripping, and if it keeps on raining you know where we'll end up—we'll end up with these eight loads tied to a bunch of cottonwood trees on some island and just awonderin when the whole island is gonna start south, barges and us and all."

"I been double-tripping since I was twenty years old," I said. "There ain't any novelty there."

"How's the new deck hand?" Casey asked.

"Him and a razor have yet to get acquainted," I says. "He claims he is seventeen, but he looks like one of the cast out of a Our Gang comedy. His mother works up at the Elite. His brother, so he told me six times, is bellhop over to the hotel. The Kid's buddy is messboy on the *Whitney* and has been giving the Kid the old River Romance stuff, I guess; anyway he seems to be bit pretty bad."

"I got the poorest T-bone I ever got in my life up there at the Elite one time. Positively worst steak I ever paid good money for."

"The Kid might make it," I said. "Anyway he ain't no weakling. Little bit skinny is all."

"There's more rain up in Wisconsin," he said. "We're gonna have enough water for everybody to have all he wants."

"If she won't shove them we'll tie off," I said. "Plenty trees between here and the Robert Street bridge in St. Paul, Minnesota."

"You better go over on the other watch tomorrow," he said, "and leave me have Jackoniski."

"A nice treat for you," I said.

"I'm not thinkin of me," he said. "I've got an idea Ironhat would better have you though. The Mate is suppose to stand the Pilot's watch anyways, not the Captain's. We been doing it this way up till now, but this trip you change over, see?"

"O.K. Ironhat don't seem so very relaxed and happy over this trip at that," I said.

"Who the hell is?" he said.

"You ought to be a carefree old Mate, like me, Captain," I said. "I ain't got a care in the world."

"Tell that to the Coast Guard," he says.

We got the tow made up in an hour or so. I had the Kid come out and get in the game but had him mostly stand back and watch. When Charlie Waters was Mate on the *Mustang* up the Illinois River he had a new deck hand they just put aboard at Chillicothe and when they came into Brandon Road Lock Charlie had the boy out on the tow. So they jack-knifed while the kid was thinking of home and paying no attention and it was night and dark in the lock anyway, and when the boy went to step over onto the other barge why it wasn't there any more of course and he went plunk into the water and right to the bottom and never even came up once. So I watch these new boys awfully close. One of the easiest things to do on a towboat is to get killed or drowned.

It was raining all the time while we were making tow and not very much of a treat to be out in it, so we got it over as soon as we could. I left the boys on their own and went back up to the pilothouse.

"Well, we are shoving 'em, anyway," Casey said, and threw his light over onto the shore.

We were shoving about two miles an hour, or less.

"After we get above the mouth of the Illinois we'll do better maybe," I said. "If we get up there by Labor Day, that is."

"We must be makin about one and a half, what do you think?" he said.

"That or a little better," I said.

"SAY MEN REMEMBER," says the radio. "Every plump luscious bean in every can of Bangs Old Style Beans is just chock full o' goodness. Yes sir, men, you'll say they're like the kind o' home-tasty beans good ole Mom used to make. So today . . ."

"My old mother couldn't cook beans or nothing else," Casey says. "That is one hell of a poor bean advertisement from my point of view."

Up above Alton the bluffs rise up on the east side of the river and at night they are dark. In the daytime they are limestone with trees at the bottom and shrubs and cedar trees hanging on the face of the cliffs, but at night the bluffs are just a big black shadow. Now if you are riding in the pilothouse on the company, getting a free vacation, it would look as though the pilot was crazy heading up into the dark, but to somebody who has been sitting around watching them do it as long as I have it is merely nothing.

"I won't call Jackoniski out until tomorrow then," I said. "I'll lay down and get a little nap until we get up to Cap au Gris, and put him on the forward watch tomorrow A.M."

"You lay down," Casey said. "I'll leave you alone unless we bust the whole works up."

"Don't talk silly," I said. "You ain't gonna bust nothing up."

"Some river coming down at us, Duke," Casey said, and I laid down on the old wicker couch at the back end of the pilothouse and took my cap with the two stars on it off and set it on the deck beside me, took off my shoes and dropped them on the deck, rolled up my blanket-lined denim jacket for a pillow, and tried to go to sleep.

"Do you think we'll get these eight loads upriver, Cap?" I said, looking at Casey's outline in the dark.

"Go to sleep," he said. "Leave all that worrying to me. I get paid for it."

"By god I hope it gets done with the idea of raining up in Wisconsin and Minnesota forever," I said.

"Go the hell to sleep," Casey said.

I laid there but I couldn't sleep, in spite of the fact that I had been up most of the night before with Lucille, loving and talking and acting the fool, and getting out of bed to stand in the window and look at St. Louis in the night.

"Ain't you never coming to bed again?" she said. "What in the world are you looking at?"

"St. Louis, Missouri," I said.

"Not much to it," she said. "You better lay down and get some sleep. You have to go back to work tomorrow."

"In a minute," I said, looking out at the city, and I went to the bathroom and poured myself another shot in a water tumbler although I didn't need one.

She was asleep again and I stood there and looked down at the street and a lonesome cab at the corner, and over the roofs and I wondered what in hell it was all about—the barge line and Lucille and me, and the tile bathroom behind me, and whoever was staying up all night down at the power-house to make the electric lights go.

"You think that new deck hand is gonna make it?" Casey said, striking a match under the pilot's chair.

"I'm asleep," I said.

Lucille was a little bit asleep and I went from the window and sat down on the edge of the bed, making it squeak, and took her hand and held it and looked over at the square of the window, pale with the lights from the street and the city. Somebody in the next room put a quarter in the radio and music came through the wall.

"Come to bed," Lucille said, very sleeplike.

"I will," I said, thinking of tomorrow and the boat and my cabin with Jackoniski, and the barges loaded with coal ahead of the boat, and the long trip upriver to St. Paul. Now she was really asleep and I went over and stood by the window with the warm tumbler in my hand and looked out the window again.

After a while of looking at St. Louis I put the tumbler down empty on the writing desk with the glass top and printed notices about Club Breakfasts and Laundry Service under it, and got in bed. I kissed Lucille and rolled over and was asleep myself.

When I woke up I smelled cigar smoke and that meant Ironhat, and I knew that the watch had changed and it was some time after midnight. I was stiff from sleeping on that hard old couch. I took a cigarette from my shirt pocket and lit it.

"Where are we?" I said.

"Going up the goddam river," Ironhat said.

"What part of the goddam river are we in, Sunshine?" I said. "Can you see that old Cap au Gris lock yet? Did we pass Grafton yet? How are we doing? Can you see the First National Bank of St. Paul?"

"I get a big kick out of your big buddy Grease Cup and his old lady," says the Ironhat. "You see him on the boat down here with them two big engines of his you would figure he was quite a big sensible man, but anytime he gets home there in St. Louis the old lady why she has him running around pissing in a tomato can; it sure beats the hell out of me, a man like him with a heavy license like what he has got, leaving some ole two-bit girl from out on the edge of town lead him around by the nose. When you come right down to it old Grease Cup is not too bad a looking man except for the country clothes, and he has a real license on diesel; a man

like Grease Cup could get a better woman than that ole
faded-out blonde movie fan. I was out to their apartment
one night she says to me, she says . . ."

"Where are we at anyway?" I said, shivering from waking
up in the April pilothouse at 1:00 A.M. It gets so mighty
chilly out here in the Middle West in the springtime after
dark. First it is winter and they are breaking ice with a couple of chartered boats up the Illinois River trying to keep
the coal moving into Chicago to Commonwealth Edison and
the others, and the deck hands when they come into Dresden
Island Lock they put on two sweatshirts under their sheep-
lined coats and they still freeze to death waiting for the
lock tenders to get the big cakes of ice unstuck so they can
open the gates—and then it is spring and the ice goes out
and in the evening the boys and girls stroll down town for
a hot fudge sundae, but after midnight take it from me out
on the river it is cold after midnight until well into May or
sometimes even June.

"Well if you want to know—" says Ironhat in the dark,
switching on the starboard searchlight and picking out a
buoy with it—"we are at Slim Island and coming up on Grafton and the Illinois River. So far as Cap au Gris is concerned
we'll be there in about four years."

"What?" I says. "The watch changed and we are not even
past Illinois River yet?"

"Didn't you hear about the high water?" Ironhat says.
"Here, hold her a minute while I go get my jacket, it is more
than a bit cool up here tonight."

I steered our eight loads up the Mississippi for him. I
picked up two black cans over to the left side with the light
and held her up on some light, Grafton Light it must have
been. No danger of running onto some trouble, we were
going so slow.

Ironhat came back and slammed the pilothouse door and took a drink of water out of the cooler.

"She ain't shoving too good," I said, turning over the steering bars to him.

"No, and she ain't going to shove any better the further we go," he said. "But I sure get a kick out of your Grease Cup and his old lady, why a man like that is perfectly crazy to put up with any such a thing."

"I will go along with you partly on that idea," I said. "I don't want no woman myself. I mean I don't want to marry none. But maybe it's good for Grease Cup. I don't know."

What the hell do I know? I don't know nothing actually, not even how to fit a truss on some union boss from the planing mill.

RADIO: . . . and now for your listening pleasure we'll twirl the disc on the ever-popular Guy Lombardo in his rendition of that perpetual favorite "April Showers."

IRONHAT: Oh Jesus! For your listening pleasure you mush-mouth these musical April Showers are giving us one great big hellish Flood over here.

ME: Come on, Carmen, leave us hear the vocals.

IRONHAT: This flood we are running up onto don't seem to bother you none.

ME: I am only a poor old Mate. If the whole works flops over I just swim ashore and thumb a ride to St. Louis. I don't feel a damn bit nervous. I don't have to lose my license if *you* hit some bridge like the *Natchez* and turn her over."

"Don't talk about the *Natchez*," he says.

They never got anybody out of the *Natchez*—she is still on the bottom with everybody inside her, in over ninety feet of water. And she's gonna stay right there too, those boys down there are gonna be steamboatin into eternity with no shore leave at all. Naturally it is a painful subject to the other pilots.

"I ain't talking about her," I says. "I'm talking about me."

"Listen, Duke," he says. "For my drinking pleasure go down and make us a pot of coffee and shut up about the *Natchez*."

"You mean some of that zestful, home-tasty coffee like good ole Mom use to make?"

"That's just the kind I mean," Ironhat said.

"One thing about us boys on the steamboats anyway, we are rich," I says. "We don't have to save the wrappers off the oranges for the kids to have toilet paper."

"Yeah, ain't we rich though," says Ironhat. "Make us a pot of coffee."

"Did the boys get up? Where are they?" I said.

"They checked the lights out on the tow an hour ago and I ain't seen them since. I imagine for their loafing pleasure they are either asleep in the deckroom or playin poker."

"That old Grease Cup," I said, getting up and putting my cap on. "He sure bothers you don't he?"

"He don't bother me none compared wth this here river and these eight lousy loads of coal," Ironhat said, shoving his chair back and standing and lighting a new cigar. "Damn," he said. "It is only 2:15 A.M. and I feel like I had been up here for about ten or a hundred hours already."

"Oh you worry too much," I said. "You ought to get a job driving a truck into Chicago and relax."

"We got a tree jammed in between the lead barges. When you get back up here with that coffee I'll back the son of a bitch and see if she'll come loose. You better get out there and see what happens. This old goddam boat ain't steering at all."

I went down and the deck hands were making fried-egg sandwiches.

"We got a tree stuck between the head barges," I said. "After I make Ironhat some coffee we'll go out there. He's gonna give her a kick back and we'll see what happens. He claims she won't steer."

"I wouldn't doubt she won't steer with some old tree in the tow," says Arkansaw. "Why wait on the coffee?" he says. "Less go out and get that old tree out between the barges right now. This here stage of water it wouldn't surprise me none if we had a whole island jammed in between the loads. Nice deal steering all them loads *without* the benefits of no tree stuck in between."

I looked up at the clock over the oil-fired stove and it said 2:23 A.M. We are always out doing some foolish thing at 2 o'clock in the morning. That makes us feel real romantic and like in the books about being up on the yardarms for three solid days froze half to death coming around Cape Horn on the *Parma* or the *Passat* or one of them books by Alan Villiers I am always getting out of the Public Library. Any of those boys that went out to sea and tortured themselves for three years on a whaler or around the Cape with no heat in the bunkroom and nothing to eat except salt pork and moldy beans and bread with bugs in it, why they could all have got a job as hired man on the farm, but that didn't appeal to their imagination somehow. Same with this old steamboating, it may keep you up late and it may get you out in a lot of Cape Horn weather sometimes for hours at a time, but anyways one thing guaranteed is it won't bore you to death.

*He's a mighty good pilot even if he does chew
Copenhagen.*

—DANNY

5

Now bear in mind all this time that we are getting
up alongside Kincaid County, which is famous for several
reasons, most of them being because of the ignorance of the
inhabitants but not so as they would notice it, in fact they
are all the time bragging about it—for example (a) because
it is the only county in the state of Illinois without even so
much as one foot of railroad track in it and (b) because
although this county is in the Rail Splitter's own state all the
boys that come from there are always telling you there "ain't
a nigger in the county ever stayed longer than sundown, they
run them out as soon's one shows up." This is the only place
along the Mississippi actually where things are like they were

back in the days of Tom and Huck, and along the banks up by Royal Landing and Fruitland Landing and Mackers Landing, Dixon Landing, Squaw Island, and up in there you can actually see the hound dogs laying around and some old women in poke bonnets hoeing or carrying a basket or sitting there on the end of a skiff, fishing. Have been on the boats with two or three boys who came from Kincaid County, Illinois, and the main line of conversation is the fact about the niggers. One old boy who was a striker engineer over on the Cumberland River once upon a time when I was over there for a two-trip job to Nashville he spent the entire watch telling me how bad they beat up a stray nigger that come into his little ignorant home town just by chance around sundown one evening. This boy could hardly sign X for his name, but him and his buddies sure beat hell out of that nigger because No Niggers Allowed in Kincaid County, Illinois.

Now that's right in the United States. And in the North, too.

The next question is, why any colored boy would *want* to enter Kincaid County as there are no attractions whatsoever unless you can count the ignorance as a feature. Certainly nobody without family there would ever dream of wanting to stay more than an hour and a half in spite of the pure white skin on everybody. In fact they are so goddam ornery in Kincaid County that they are mean as hell to *anybody*, even white strangers, who wander into some of them terrible crossroads. They come up and want to fight, and they egg the dogs on strangers also. They are proud of all this, too. Like those bastards down in Texas. Yeah, I been down there, too. Ten minutes is long enough.

We got up past Illinois River mouth and Masons Island and Squaw Island about 3 A.M. She didn't shove any better after we passed Illinois River and as we came up around the big bend of Kincaid County she seemed to be very sluggish and fighting the current in a heavy sort of way and steering bad also.

All these damn boats steer bad in high water anyway. It's just that you have to watch the tow, out in front of you 800 feet, a little closer and not get so excited with your own conversation or listening to the radio or thinking of times gone by and all the things you would do over if you had them to do over again that you don't pay enough attention.

I even used to get to thinking of all kinds of inconsequential things when I was on the night watch—and not pilot either—just more or less of an extra man, which is what the Mate is in between locks and landings—such as the old old stuff about home and the box elder leaves that used to blow around in the gutter in the fall of the year and the time I kissed some girl, such as Roma Schlesinger, on a punk front porch after getting off the bus after the evening show on Friday night. Not to mention walking nineteen blocks home afterwards to save a five-cent piece and looking into house after frame house all dark, except maybe one or two with the old man sitting there reading James Oliver Curwood or the *American Magazine* or the *Collected Works of O. Henry* under the living-room lamp with the beaded fringe around the shade.

God knows what Ironhat was ever thinking of hour after hour from midnight until 6 A.M. as he called for one cup of coffee after another and the invisible shores of the Upper Mississippi slid past on either side in the dark.

Or anybody else aboard for that matter. Down in the engine room was this misfit Kennedy with his baking soda, a good engineer when it came to actually getting the most out of two enormous diesel engines, but not adjusted to ding-donging up and down the river at all. What was his trouble? He kept quiet about it so none of us knew. All we knew about Kennedy, and hell, we didn't care much because he was so

bad off the beat to start with, was that he was mad at everything.

Jackoniski? Oh the hell with that lousy crumb. He was
the type who would kick your head off if somebody gave
him twenty-five cents for the job, and probably entertained
himself torturing small animals when he was out in the
country. With all that after-shave lotion he used and the
suit with the stripes on it and the neatly folded silk pocket
handkerchief he had a lot of nice clean-cut girls thinking
he was O.K. and that was a big mistake. But what was in his
head? Nothing except meanness, I suppose.

And then the Grease Cup—our chief engineer on whom we
all depended to get up the river in record time and deliver
our coal to the customers and secure us a large bonus, now
what in the world was in the Cup's head all this time? Just
more misery from the old lady. But he also loved those two
Superior engines.

Naturally I didn't get anything done on my Correspondence Course that first night out of St. Louis, what with the
high water and changing over to the other watch, and the
Kid coming aboard, and the darkness of it all and worrying
about things, in spite of my nice talk about being a Carefree
Mate. Some boys don't worry. I never worried on any other
job I was ever on, as far as that goes, and I don't actually
worry on the steamboats, but I *care*, as they say on the soap
operas.

There was a few of us on the boat who cared: Casey, I
think, and the Grease Cup, and old Swede, and One Eye,
and Clarence with his liquid logumberry pies, and possibly
one of the wipers, but wipers are so low in the social scale
they don't count and they might just as well not be aboard
at all except for the comic relief when somebody pours syrup
in their shoes when they are asleep or something like that.

"What is your name, boy?" the Grease Cup used to say

once in a while to some wiper who had been struggling on-ward and upward in the engine room for months. Which shows that the Cup was not without his dirty side, too. As who isn't? But he didn't do it very often, and most of the time he was like a daddy to the lone wiper on his watch. When he did say it, it was only in fun. I have even seen the Grease Cup buy his wiper a beer in the tavern down on Marceau Street in St. Louis, near the shipyards, after stand-ing square watches in dry dock for three days.

You can beat some son of a bitch over the head uptown and get no work out of him but give him a job on the water and he will do the damnedest things in order nobody will think he is a quitter. You can tell anybody to do anything, nearly, on a boat, and they will do it. They figure they have to break their neck for the team for some reason, which it says is Psychology in the Correspondence Course and maybe it is. Whatever it is, you can drive a man harder on a boat than you can anyplace on the shore.

We went out and tried to get the tree out from in between the barges, but we couldn't do it. Ironhat would roll her back and we would turn the side lines loose, but the barges never will come apart when you want them to (and always when you don't).

"Look, ve passing Kincaid County," the Swede said to Arkansaw. "They don't leave no niggers . . ."

"Yeah, yeah," says Arkansaw, who was a loose-jointed old boy who only shaved once a week. "I reckon I been by here a million times. I done heard all about it. All about it."

Old Hank Bunker done it once, and bragged about it; and in less than two years he got drunk and fell off of the shot tower, and spread himself out so that he was kind of a layer, as you may say . . .

—HUCK

6

AGE creeps up on us when we are not looking, when we are doing a lot of things that are a lot of miserable foolishness such as taking correspondence courses, reading up on how to make yourself a swell backyard barbecue fireplace, turning the pages of *True Confessions* magazine, or working all day and being too tired in the evening to do anything but argue. You play pool and join the Eagles or the Moose Club, and you get your hair cut, and the seasons change and it rains and snows and the birdies go tweet tweet; then you find yourself in the men's room of some forty-nine cent Middle West night club, inhaling the perfume of the West Disinfecting Co.'s urinal deodorant, and when you look at yourself in the mirror as you arrange your curly locks with an Ace pocket comb you realize that you are old, and mean as hell, and you wonder where the years went to so sudden.

Already I was thirty-three years old and if that seems like a poor time to squawk about being too old just figure how old the Kid looked on me, he figured I was around seventy-five by comparison. I knew everything, you see, and he knew nothing. That is not so funny because actually I did; it just takes a very few years of bumming around to change you from a kid to a sour old man in this country or any other country or possibly even in outer space on Altair or Benetnasch or Regulus, which I am acquainted with as well as others from working nights with another captain, named Putnam. No, there is such a short time between being scared and wondering how to purchase a ticket to Sioux City, and then all of a sudden knowing too much about tickets, trains, and especially Sioux City. Once upon a time you are a little bit shy about asking some girl to accompany you to the dance following the basketball game with East Moline, and then before you know it there are girls all over the place: redheads, brunettes, blondes, mouseheads; and trailer camps, hotel rooms, culverts, back rooms, front rooms, couches, day beds, folding cots, eiderdown sleeping bags, back alleys, sand bars, willow groves, two-room flats; there are sunrises not as sweet as you would want, and trips to the drugstore for some of those pills, and there are wonderful girls that pull your hair and love the hell out of you and others that sit forever in taverns telling about the time they went to the hospital and how nice everybody was, and what funny things they said when they come out of the ether.

"That Kid he will end up getting killed on this boat," the Grease Cup said.

"No he won't," I said. "Any more than you or I did."

"You better keep your eye on him then."

"I ain't going to keep my eye on nothing," I says, "except the progress of this outfit up the river. Anyway Casey changed me over onto the after watch. So the Kid has got Jackoniski to work for. I can't worry about that."

"That's a bad deal for the Kid," says the Cup.

"What the hell is everybody so worried about this goofy kid from Alton for?" I said. "He come aboard just like I did ten years ago. Nobody tried to spare me no unhappy times."

"Yeah," says the Grease Cup. "I know. I was there myself one time."

Naturally I was watching this boy on account of the initial oration he had given me up on the bank that night in the dark down at Alton. He was struck crazy by the idea of going out on the river, and all of us bums when we see somebody young that has the fever why we look on them with a much more kindly eye than just the usual floaters that come out on the river for free bed and board and would be just as happy on some construction job in Kansas.

"Why," says I, "is everybody worked up into such a sweat over this here Kid?"

"I don't know," says the Grease Cup. "He is kind of a comical Kid. And he sure tries to please. That in itself is quite a novelty."

"He's got to make it on his own," I said. "*I* ain't going to do him no goddam favors for sure. Nobody ever done me any."

"Yeah," says the Grease Cup, spitting into the river outside the engine-room door. "You're a hard-boiled old goat, ain't you? You ain't paying no attention to the Kid at all, I can tell that. My you are a tough one."

So the next evening after supper I was sitting in the pilot-house before going to bed (I was all balled up on my sleeping and living arrangements since getting changed over to the After Watch) and talking to friend Casey in his gray felt hat, and looking more like a refrigerator salesman in Famous Barr or some other St. Louis store, and I was looking over the evening sky and the willows and elm trees about to bust into leaf on the islands, when there came a *knock*, of all things, on the pilothouse door and receiving no answer, the Kid came in. He took off his cap and closed the door and stood there like a spring lamb on Wabash Avenue and he says, "Well, as a matter of fact it seems kinda silly to me, but the Mate told me he says I am to come up here and check the whistle."

"He did did he?" says Casey.

"Yes, sir, that's what he tole me," says the Kid standing there very skinny and wanting to be a big help. "It might be he is playing a joke on me, but on the other hand I have to do what he says and like Maw says to me, 'When you go out on the boat now Delbert,' she says, 'you have to do what they tell you every time or you won't never get to be the captain no matter how long you stay.' 'O.K., Maw,' I says to her, and it's really a shame the way they work her over there to the Elite, seventy-five cents an hour ain't nothing like what she is worth and my brother he could help out some but he don't. He is a good enough boy but runs around too much in that Model-A Ford of his and he is always off with some girl or . . ."

"Wait a minute. Slack off, boy," says Casey.

"Take it easy, Kid," I says. "Slow down."

"Now where did you get the fancy gauntlets?" Casey says, for the Kid is standing there with a pair of Big American gloves on, the kind they soak you $1.85 for in any of the stores in Alton or St. Louis.

"Why Mr. Grease Cup lended me these here gloves," the Kid said. "He said I could pay him back off my first pay check. He said I couldn't go to work deckin out there on the barges without a proper pair of gloves. My buddy over on the

Wheelock Whitney he never tole me what I should bring
along and neither did that man up there at the *e*mployment
office. Brother Tim he tole me when I went up to the hotel
where he is head bellhop at and tole him I had got the job
he says, 'Listen, Delbert,' he says. 'Things are agoing to be
just one hell of a lot different than what you think they are
when you actually get out there on Old Man River, you are
going to find out probly that you have got all the wrong
stuff with you and the other boys on the job are agoing to
just raise hell with you, buddy.' I thought he was trying to
disencourage me off the job but I see already Tim was about
half right. Anyway this Mr. Grease Cup who runs the motors
down there is a mighty friendly man and he give me these
here gloves."

"What caused you to stop talking?" says Casey.

"I ain't got no more to say, I guess," says the Kid.

When the Kid begun one of these speeches of his we all
shut up and looked at him and each other until he was
through, never knowing what in hell was coming next. For
example, he is always calling the engines the "motors," which
affords us all a general laugh, but for some reason we never
lit on the Kid and straightened him out and explained on
what points he was wrong, we just left him ramble on; it was
better than having a Wurlitzer jukebox aboard.

"These here gloves that Mr. Grease Cup give me is just the
kind of a pair gloves I always wanted. With the big cuffs,"
says our boy.

"Yeah, you're a killer in them gloves," Casey said.

"Go on down and find the rest of the boys, Kid," I said.
"The Mate just sent you up here to try to make a fool of you,
but pay no attention to that and just go back down and tell
them you checked the whistle and everything is O.K."

So he went away and we were shoving our eight loads
over so slow upstream and all the water out of Minnesota,

Wisconsin and Iowa was coming down the valley at us. It was 6:30 P.M. and cool outside and very overcast and a mournful sky and we were creeping up the river so slow you would figure it was down on the Lower Mississippi in springtime. We were only at Schwanigan Island Light and still twenty miles below Clarksville. I felt like going down to my bunk and reading up on my Correspondence Course, or at least some story in *Collier's* which would take me far far away from the mighty motor vessel *Royal Prince*, but instead I sat there after the Kid had gone away, looking up the broad valley and over the scrubby islands. It was dusk and Casey had the radio going. Somebody was working on a violin. Casey didn't say anything and neither did I and we just sat there with the whole Mississippi Valley in flood all around us, with fence posts and trash floating down, and the current rushing over the small islands and through the willow clumps, flattening them down and making them wiggle with the water tearing past them. Over on our right there was an old shackly frame house on stilts with the water up near the floor and a long unpainted flatboat tied up to it with the registration number painted on in big crooked letters. Up on the roof there was a little old scrub fox terrier running from side to side and looking down to see when somebody would remember he was up there. There was smoke coming out of the stovepipe on the house, so you could see these people were sticking it out even with their house about to slide over on its side any minute and start down-river for Cape Girardeau and points further south.

"Look," Casey said. "Them silly fools over there ain't got the sense to get out."

"Maybe the crest is past," I said.

"Maybe the crest ain't got here yet neither," he said.

Some drunk in a bar down in St. Louis had given me a

cigar and I had been moving it around from shirt to shirt and now I took it out and lit it, but it wouldn't draw.

"Some swell cigar," I said. "It won't draw and I can't get so much as a puff off her."

"Probly bent," Casey said, so I cut it in two with my jack-knife and smoked one half of it, which worked O.K.

"If we don't tie into a swell fog we'll be up at Clarksville around 5 A.M.," Casey said.

Violin music. And the dusk began to thicken down.

"My sister use to play the violin," Casey said after quite a while, during which I said nothing and all the sound was the windows of the pilothouse rattling a little bit, with the vibration of the boat—although we had all kinds of little wedges that we used to whittle with our pocketknives (while sitting around the pilothouse) and stick in the sash to keep them quiet—and the violin playing and making everybody want to bust out crying.

"She could have gone ahead with her violin," Casey said, as a few ducks going north settled down behind a sand point over to the east.

The fact of Casey being related to the human race surprised me—much less a sister, who I saw standing in the front parlor with pigtails, sawing away on some piece called "Reverie" or "Meditation."

"She could of gone places on the violin," he said, pushing his hat back and lighting another of ten million cigarettes he had smoked in his time.

"What caused her to give it up?" I said, feeling something was necessary although embarrassed at even getting into this conversation because Casey was never one to let on he had a muscle or a nerve in his body, let alone feelings and violinist members of the family.

"Oh hell, she run off with some runt from Indiana," Casey said. "I ain't seen Grace in twenty-five years. Man how she could play that violin when she was only fourteen years old. She was the pride and joy of old Professor Meyer."

"Did you ever see the Rocky Mountains from Denver?" I said after a while. "That is something you don't forget so quick."

"Hell, yes, I have," Casey said. "But why bring that up? Here we are out steamboating on the Upper Mississippi on a very poor night in April and take it from me it is going to start raining before midnight. And by the way why don't you get into the friendly sack and get some rest?"

"Well I am so used to the forward watch it just seems unnatural to me as hell to be getting into bed at 7 P.M., but I think I will accept your suggestion and do it anyway," I said.

"I wish you would change this new boy over onto your watch," Casey said. "I am afraid Jackoniski will stick it into him and break it off. You know how Jackoniski is."

"Yeah. I shave outa the same bowl," I said. "I knew him years before I ever met him anyway. I knew him up in Iowa and I knew him out on the plains—there is always some —— like Jackoniski around no matter where you go."

"This here Kid is a natural fool—no doubt about that—but on the other hand . . ."

"On the other hand why don't you stake him to a pair of good shoes now that Grease Cup has fixed him up with gloves? And I will get him a innerspring mattress for his bunk, so he don't have to suffer like the rest of the boys. What has come over everybody on this boat anyway? Here we are coming upriver on a stage of high water and every conversation ends up on this goofy kid from Alton."

"When was you ever in Denver inspecting the Rocky Mountains," Casey said.

"*Say men,*" says the radio, "have you got Razor-Blade Skin? Now's the time to change to . . ."

"I bummed all over the West before I went crazy and come out here steamboating," I said. "Why, Captain, I was fourth bus boy in the Brown Palace Hotel for three weeks one time. Talk about violin music . . ."

The pilothouse door opened and Jackoniski came in and slouched down in one of the wicker chairs and began to pick his teeth with his pocketknife.

"Well I believe I will get a little sleep," I said, getting up to go.

"Don't leave me interrupt your high-tone conversations," Jackoniski said.

"Don't forget to have the deck hand wake me up at 11:30," I said with my hand on the doorknob.

"Never fear about that," he said.

"Get some sleep, Duke," Casey said. "It is still raining up in Minnesota."

I went down to the galley because I was in no mood to sleep. I don't know what was the matter with me on this trip but I couldn't seem to get settled down in the old bunk with a good magazine and take it easy when I was off watch, I was getting out of bed and looking out the window two or three times and drinking more coffee than usual, which is around nineteen cups per minute.

The stove was turned down way low so I opened up the valve a little and set a pot of coffee on and took out my keys and found the one to the big brass padlock on the freezer and opened the door. I walked into the cold box and got

Some Cocktail Fruit with no cherries
7   Prunes in a Dish
2   slices Liverwurst on a cracked plate
½ can Dark Sweet Cherries
2½ Peach Halves in Syrup.

I was working on these and toasting myself some toast

when the Kid come in the door with his gauntlet gloves on that the Grease Cup had donated him.

"How do you like it now?" I said to him.

"I like it fine," he said. "I am suppose to bring the Mate a cup of coffee."

"I am the Mate and he is the Second Mate," I said. "Now just where is he that he is sending you around the boat to bring him coffee? Where is he, playing poker, I suppose, with the deck hands and the cook."

"All this is real different than I thought it was going to be," says the Kid.

"Yeah," I says, "and it will get more different every minute you stay aboard. There is hardly a thing you can name that is more different than working on one of these bum old towboats trying to shove a bunch of coal from Illinois up to Minnesota."

"The Second Mate he says no sugar and about a tablespoonful of milk in his coffee will be about right."

"Well you be sure you get it just right for him," I said. "We don't want no mistakes on Jackoniski's coffee order."

"I know it," says the Kid.

So I went up and climbed into the sack and just as I was going in my door up on the boiler deck a drop of rain hit me on the forehead like a message from up above someplace. I was beginning to get where I didn't care a damn and I went right to sleep after laying there in the dark for a few minutes, listening to the engines and smoking a lousy cigarette. I had that dream for a while—that dream I have been having for twenty years or more—I am standing out on the sidewalk back in the home town, late in the fall of the year; it is night and some reason or other I am always aware of a big dark blue sky filled with stars. I am standing there on the sidewalk, looking across a yard with a house there, and there is a big window and behind the plate glass there is this big domestic scene, like the advertisements for Oil Burners, with a couple of tiny tots playing with their dolls on the genuine Wilton carpet and Papa has the baby on his lap and Mama is setting on the overstuffed davenport, knitting somebody a sweater. Then this hellish big police dog comes charging out from the side of the house and comes charging out in my direction and the dream ends with me running down the street.

I've had that dream two or three times a year since I was about fifteen years old. Maybe the psychologists can make something out of it.

It always wakes me up.

I got up and had a drink of water and leaned out the door of my cabin for a minute. It was 9 P.M. by my watch. It had settled down to a steady cold spring rain.

And then we murdered the bos'un tight, And
he much resembled pig;

—W. S. GILBERT

7

JUST so you will know let me tell you a few facts about what it is like on the romantic Upper Mississippi in the early navigation season in spring, when it has been snowing like hell all winter up North and the thaws are bringing the run-off down to the Gulf of Mexico.

Up in Minneapolis all those houseboats tied off down under the hill by the University of Minnesota—which look so picturesque on a June or an August afternoon—bust loose their moorings and pile up someplace upside down. Squatters who live below the Ford Dam hightail it for town and sit around the taverns while the photographers from the *St. Paul Post-Dispatch* charter boats and go out and take pictures of the water going over the roofs of their shanties or rolling same shanties into trees. Some dog or cat gets caught by the flood on a roof and is rescued and that solves the human-interest story for the Twin Cities papers for that day.

The water rises and rises and where you could play horseshoes under the elm trees on the islands at Wabasha or Red Wing or Lansing last summer there is a million gallons of water six feet deep and overturning trees and cabins and washing banks and wing dams and whole islands, little ones, away. The people in Winona and La Crosse and Hastings drive their cars past the levee in the evenings and look at the flood and go home or over to the moving-picture show. Any animals that got trapped on the islands in the raise climb into the trees, or swim ashore, or drown and go floating down the river with the driftwood and trees and loose boards and bottles and beer cans and front porches and orange crates and oil drums and planks and derelict skiffs and vinegar jugs.

"The most patheticest part of the Ohio River flood in 1937 was the animals," the Grease Cup used to say. "The human beings was bad enough, but the animals, say, they had a bad time of it and I don't mean maybe. We picked up every kind of animal you ever heard of and they was all starved to death and so weak they couldn't move a muscle. By god they had guts though. They would swim until they died, hogs and all. But you know a hog is a very poor swimmer."

I didn't know it, but I'll believe it.

The flood does not quit when the sun goes down over the river valley, it gets worse at night if anything. All night long while the cops in the river towns stop their squad cars at the Busy Bee Café for coffee or try the door latches in the industrial districts, and while the train dispatchers and railroad telegraphers smoke cigarettes and listen to the rattle of the key, the flood keeps on coming down from Minnesota, and from Wisconsin, out of all the little rivers nobody ever heard of, dumping into the Mississippi, and up she goes, and the bridge tenders call home on the telephone and say, "I am O.K., honey. This bridge went through sixteen floods already and it is solid as a rock. It is sure not going out tonight. How is the baby, did she go to sleep yet?"

The driftwood and busted-up boats and pieces of floating shanties pile up on the upstream ends of the towheads, and uptown everybody on the flats anywhere down near the river is running pumps to keep the water out of the cellar and when the water comes up into the front yard and then into the living room they move the furniture upstairs. The police and the Coast Guard come up the street now in boats and tie up to the front porch and there is always some old girl ninety-five years old who refuses to go and has to be carried out, or a fat boy weighing four hundred pounds who is lugged out by six men and taken to the Armory where they have set up cots. All the school kids line up and have typhoid shots because the water system is all messed up. The newsreels send in cameramen and sound trucks. All the stores are sold out of rubber boots and sump pumps. The railroads give up, and then at night it is very still except for the sound of gasoline pumps blasting away all night long. The Red Cross comes to town. Somebody writes a letter to the paper and explains the flood is caused by the Locks and Dams. Somebody else writes back and says the Weyerhauser Lumber Co. is to blame for cutting off all the lumber eighty years ago.

One interesting sight you will always see in the flood time between St. Louis and St. Paul, those two popular Saints, is the brakemen on the railroad out in rubber boots, and the freight trains moving so slow they are just barely moving, for fear the ballast has washed out under the ties. You also can see colored boys off the section gang walking the tracks in hip boots, with sticks, and feeling the switches under water to see if they are clear or not.

"Thanks"—I remember hearing an old boy we picked off an island below Muscatine tell the cook one night on the *Transporter*—"that the Almighty invented coffee whilst He was making the world out of mud or whatever it was He done it with."

During the high water the demand for coffee increases to the point where sometimes you are drinking eighteen cups every six hours and can't sleep off watch no matter how tired you are from relief work and sandbagging, or even from standing around looking important and giving orders to a few people who will then hate you forever.

"Ifn I didn't have to get up at midnight I do blieve I'd have another mug of coffee," said the sweet-smelling deck hand as he finished his fourth cup at 8 P.M. and renched it out in the zink.

Once when I was a kid a big freight engine, creeping slowly along with the water over the cowcatcher, and making waves like a boat, slid over on its side and blew up the boiler, and the train crew's family were a neighborhood sensation for twenty-four hours what with the floral offerings, casket arrangements, relatives in from the country to see the remains, and out-of-state cars parked in front of the house.

Bearing in mind, friends, that I am talking about high water up above St. Louis (or Cairo, to be exact) because down on the lower end it is really one sweet mess when they have high water: for example, it floods way back into the country down there, all over the farms (such as they are), and everybody—not only those who live down by the river but also folks who are peacefully farming way back—has to get up on the roof and wait for the rescue boats to come along, and sometimes Grandma gets hung up in a treetop, or the house overturns before the Coast Guard or anybody can get there and everything is lost, including the new fifty-three-piece set of dishes, as well as a number of lives.

"Was you ever up the Illinois on a good flood stage?" says the Grease Cup. "Well we sunk the good old *Gloria* up there at Marseilles and it was right in broad daylight too," he said as we were standing around as usual by the engine-room door on the shore side. "We raised her a few days later, but a deck hand named Novak never got off in time and when we got her up there he was, layin in his bunk as peaceful as hell or more so, with two inches of Illinois River crap over the blanket. Not a very wonderful sight by a long shot I'm here to admit. Layin there he was, like he was sound asleep, and he had been dead and under the Illinois River about sixteen feet for four days. Was you ever up the Illinois in high water, Duke?"

"I been everyplace," I said. "Didn't you know I been everyplace? And I never missed no high water yet. And the Illinois is just as mean or maybe meaner than the rest."

"Mean? Why, man, I was up in there on the *Red Cloud* one time in the flood of 1943 we come up in there above Morris and there was so much water coming down the river that Captain Edwards he decide to tie up; so we got four good lines out and thank God we got them onto some good trees because six hours later the water was up two feet more and, believe me or not, to keep from going downstream on the flood we put two more good three-inch Manila lines out to hold our loads down and then we cut the boat loose. You see, Edwards wasn't so dumb although rather a prohibitionist, Volstead's right-hand man so to speak, and he figured if the loaded barges got carried away, why on a flood like that there wouldn't be nothing the boat could do anyways so might as well tie off separate and at lease save the boat. Well I was all hot then on being a steam engineer," the Grease Cup said, stroking his nose and looking sober, "and

I was aboard, of all things, to get steam license and working as striker although I had my diesel license at the time. I was told many a time that I was out of my head to want steam license. They told me steam was done, even my old lady she climbed all over me on the very same subject. The way it turned out, of course she and all of them was right. Anyways we run up a few hunnerd yards above the loads and tied off and, believe it or not, Duke my boy, but in four hours we was running the engines full head, just to keep from getting carried away. We had four big Manila lines out, but man were they taking a strain. We run that old paddlewheel between half and full head all night long and all the next day. I can't say I done no sleeping off watch. I just set in the messroom and drunk coffee when I wasn't in the engine room."

"Ironhat don't like this deal at all," I said, leaning on the door frame and looking out into the dark, but feeling the high water and the drowned islands all around us. Over on the islands that we couldn't see, who knows how many kids was clinging to the chimney and crying while all the livestock washed off down the river, kicking and squirming, even the very poor swimming hogs.

"Ironhat is smart if he don't like it," the good old Grease Cup said, pulling a toothpick out of the breast pocket of his blue chambray shirt and dislodging a piece of pot roast from molar number seven. "Anybody who wants to get out and fool around on the Mississippi River in high water who don't have to is plumb crazy."

"That about covers the description of all of us," I said.

"Yes, I guess we have all got a few bolts loose," says the Cup. "We none of us have to be here unless we want to."

"It must be we crave excitement, like them old pioneers," I said. "I suppose we are here just on account of the flood. All of us have probably just been waiting for the high water, when you come right down to it. None of us knew it when we come, but we've been waiting for it."

"What about the Kid?"

"Him too," I said. "There's a high-water boy if I ever seen one."

"Well he come to the right place if he wants adventure," says Cup. "He sure picked a daisy for his first go at steamboating."

"Let me tell you about Kincaid County, Illinois," I said. "They don't leave no niggers . . ."

"So I heard," he said.

So then it begun to rain again, down where we were, and all up the valley and out onto the rolling plains of Iowa and Minnesota, and over in America's Dairyland in Wisconsin. It began to rain clear up to Hudson's Bay, and it never wanted to stop at all, the raindrops was pattering on shed roofs and boxcars and on cattle standing in the fields, all over the Middle West.

"Well, there comes some more rain," I said.

"This is going to be good, before long," the Grease Cup said, and he turned away from the river and went into the bright shiny noisy engine room where everything was clean and neat and efficient and nothing wrong could ever happen.

Trees won't grow worth shucks in a Cincinnati graveyard, but in a Sent Louis graveyard they grow upwards of eight hundred feet high. It's all on account of the water the people drunk before they laid up. A Cincinnati corpse don't richen the soil any.

—MARK TWAIN

8

WHEN you are out on the boats you think a lot about things that are over on the land, things you never bother to think about at all when you are there. The girl problem, for one thing, becomes something you live with, and think about, and talk about. Oh man, the millions of hours that have been spent since the Egyptians or somebody invented boats, by men and boys sitting around on deck and in messrooms and bunkrooms and engine rooms talking about girls. There are a lot of topics covered but it will come around to girls almost every time, especially amongst the deck hands and wipers and other younger generation; a whole lot of your older men have had enough of the subject and some to spare, and would a whole lot rather talk about squirrel hunting.

We were sitting around the messroom in all that water up above Cap au Gris someplace. It was midnight. The boys going off watch were setting there thinking about whether to peel an orange or go to bed. The boys coming on watch were yawning and stretching and pouring coffee and blowing on it.

On the After Watch, which works twelve to six, and which I now had since Casey made the changeover, for deck hands I had Zero and Arkansaw and Swede. Zero was nothing. He was just a guy someplace between twenty-five and fifty in a pair of dirty pants and a denim jacket. He ate and slept and got up and followed the boys around and did his work all right but hardly ever said a word. He probably had less personality, so to speak, than any deck hand on the whole upper river. I don't know what he looked like.

Arkansaw on the other hand was a boy with plenty of noise. He had opinions, facts, stories, jokes, reminiscences, and when he run out of any of these just to break the silence he would whistle or play the harmonica to raise the dead. He used to tell funny stories about Arkansaw, but we will spare the reader by not listing any of them here. Frankly I can't get too much humor out of these hillbilly comics, but some people simply dote on it. Arkansaw wore bib overalls and a railroad engineer's style shop cap of blue with large white polka dots on it. He would kind of lose some of the worst of his accent after forty or fifty days on the boat; then he would come back from ten-day vacation down home and it would be so thick again you couldn't understand him at all for two or three days until it had wore off a little. He was the type that calls his wife his "waaf" and an egg an "aig" and all that crap. To us Northern boys he sounded like he had been listening to too damn many hillbilly radio programs and was just putting it on. I still think Southern people could talk like normal human beings if they wanted to, but they think it is cute to talk like that. Arkansaw also had a clasp knife with a spring blade that he was supposed to of killed somebody with down in Helena. All I can say is, I've been to Helena quite a bit on the oil tows, and he could kill two or three dozen in that town and it couldn't help but be an improvement.

The other one on my watch was the Swede. He was what the name indicates—a Swede. You no doubt know the rest. He came from the outskirts or suburbs of Two Harbors Minnesota and all his folks were Great Lakes people. He was a Great Lakeser too and went out on the ore boats when he was only a kid, but to get him to tell about it was an honest chore as he had about as much gift of gab as the average telephone pole and conversation was like drawing teeth with a pair of pliers. The Swede was a big lunkhead like all Swedes in other words, and also like all Swedes he had boats and the water built into him alongside of his blood vessels. And although a lunkhead, he was a good old lunkhead, "loyal and true," and he would work until he dropped. He was always wanting me to come up to Two Harbors. He was going to take me deer hunting and all that and I had a notion I would go sometime.

Well, that was my watch—Zero, Arkansaw, and the Swede.

"I can't make up my mind about the girls somehow," the Kid pipes up as I came into the messroom feeling ratty as hell as I have a thousand times before when I had to work this lousy midnight to six A.M. watch. I sure don't like climbing out of the sack at midnight and going to work.

"Seems like I want all of them," says the Kid, looking a little bit skinny as he was going off watch and eating a piece of bread and margarine and peanut butter, with peach jam smeared all over the top of it an inch thick.

"I'm going the hell to bed," said One Eye and went.

"I go to the show with one, it seems like she is the one I want, then there is two or three girls sitting around in the show I notice, after my eyes get use to the dark, who look better than the one I am with."

"Me for the old sack," says the Wiper on the Forward Watch with his hands all grease.

I poured me out a cup of coffee.

"After the show—" says the Kid, taking a big bite—"there is always half a dozen hanging around the drugstore who look even better."

"Yeah," says Stevie, the other deck hand beside One Eye on the Forward Watch. "I know what you mean, Kid. Golly they all look good, don't they though?" And he rolled a cigarette and went through the door into the galley for a match.

Jackoniski was sitting at the end of the table behind the red and white tablecloth with supper gravy and prune juice on it, with a sneer four and a half feet wide on his face as he busted an egg on the side of a glass and then drank it raw.

"They don't bother me none," he said. "Give them a clout over the head with a good stout club," he said. "They ain't pushin me around none."

"Anyway that's the way it goes all day long," says the Kid. "Danged if I can make up my mind."

"One is as good as another," says Jackoniski. "They are all just only good for one thing, and most of them no good for that, neither," and he went to bed.

"I wisht I was a girl so I could have a nice date with Jackoniski," says the Wiper off the Forward Watch, pouring Karo syrup on some corn flakes. "He is so lovable and romantic."

"What did you say you was doing down there in Alton before you come on the boat?" says Arkansaw, sitting down and stirring a saltine cracker in his coffee.

"Well I done a number of things," the Kid said. "I use to do yard work in the summers, and then I worked with the Midwest Roofing Co. for a while and helped send the tar up in buckets. Also worked on a farm. Then the last job I had why I was with the Winkler Fuel and Supply Company, Better Fuel for Less Money, A Fuel for Every Purse and Every Purpose. So we had a load of Pocahontas six-inch lump for an address called 1938 Riverview Avenue. We had four ton. We found the house and the coal chute and dumped the four ton into the cellar and went back to the coalyard to get orders. We no sooner got there than Ed Peavey come stormin out of the office mad as could be. 'Where did you deliver them four ton?' he said. 'Why up at 1938 Riverview,' I said. 'That's right,' said the driver I worked with, a very dumb guy named Red. 'Why you dumb damn fools,' says Peavey. 'I just got a phone call from some woman and she says she just got home and while she was gone somebody come and filled her cellar full of coal. She says she got an oil burner three years ago and don't need coal any more than the smallpox. You damn fools must a put the coal in the wrong house.' 'No we never did either,' says Red. 'No we never did either,' says Peavey giving an imitation of Red. 'Naturally somebody with an oil burner needs four ton of soft coal in their basement. You guys are fired. Leave the truck right where it stands.' I never said nothing. 'But listen . . .' says Red. 'Wait a minute,' says Peavey. 'On second thought you're hired again. Go on out to that address and carry that coal out and reload it into the truck. And don't put it in nobody else's basement, just bring it back here. Don't do nothing with that coal only load it into the truck and bring it back and we'll start over on the order,' he says. Well we climb into the truck . . ."

"Wait a minute, Kid," I said. "Slow down."

"Yeah, stop for a breath," says Arkansaw.

"I use to work for one that sounds a lot like this here Peavey," says the Wiper.

"Well go on," I said. "What happened?"

"Oh hell me and Red climb into the truck again and went back up to 1938 Riverview and we went around to the back door and was about to knock on the door to explain what it was all about when the door bust open and this skinny old lady come out aflyin and boy did she lace it into us. 'And not only that,' she says, 'but I just Kem-Toned my whole basement and now it looks like the inside of a coal mine.' She raved on and on and after a while she cooled down and we set to work shoveling that four ton of coal into coal baskets and carrying it up the cellar stairs and out to the truck. It took us most all day, with knocking off a half hour for lunch. This old girl finely took pity on us about 4 P.M. and she says, 'Well I guess it was not your fault; I imagine it was that old fool Ed Peavey was behind it all when you come right down to it,' and she brung us out each a piece of apple pie and a cup of coffee. 'Listen Ma'm,' I says, 'I will come up evenings and Kem-Tone your basement over for you. I ain't got too much to do evenings anyways.' 'No you won't,' she says. 'I done it myself last time with the aid of my husband, but this time a union painter is going to handle the job and the Winkler Fuel and Supply Company is going to pay for it.'"

"She was right about that," says the Wiper opening the peanut-butter jar and beginning to smear two dozen crackers.

"Carryin four ton of coal up out of the cellar, now that's a nice job," says Arkansaw. "No wonder you come out steamboatin."

"Did Winkler pay for the paint job?" I said. The boat began to shake and a can of cocktail fruit fell off the shelf and

lit on the deck. Nobody picked it up. It rolled over by the
door on the starboard side, the Illinois side.

"I spose so, but I don't rightly know," says the Kid, "for
when we got back to Winkler's with our load why Peavey
come out and fired us all over again. So we quit. And I
went home and I never heard no more about it."

"I reckon Winkler paid," Arkansaw said.

"They couldn't hardly do nothing else," says the Wiper.

"I vass lookin at river yust now," says the Swede, on his
third cup of coffee in ten minutes. "Ve ain't gettin noplace."

"That old girl sure was mad," the Kid said.

"You can't blame her much for that," says the Wiper with
his mouth full of peanut-butter crackers.

"The rain qvit and temperature is falling," says the Swede.
"Ve be out tying dam rig off in fog before vatch changes."

"How old was this woman who give you the pie?" says
the Wiper.

"Oh she was old. Thirty-five or forty," says the Kid.

"A regular antique," I says.

*You must break all the Commandments well in
the Western Country.*

—THE VIRGINIAN

9

THEY used to cut a range boiler lengthwise, when
I was a kid back in Minnesota, and set it in the front yard
on a gas-pipe stand for a flower box with geraniums in it.
Out in the back yard if there was a good tree they used to
make a swing with a piece of rope and an old auto tire. In
summertime they brought out the open-sided streetcars. On
Halloween the gangs used to go out and push over privies,
and there were plenty of them to push. When there was a
ball game down at the ball park a fellow used to drive a
horse and buggy up Main Street with a big umbrella over it
hollering "Baseball Today" through a megaphone. When they
had a New Year's Eve Midnight Show at the Majestic Thea-

ter the management would make a deal with the electric company to have four streetcars ready after the show to take everybody home. People made crystal sets and sat around with headphones on, listening to somebody play "The Prisoners Song" on the musical saw from WOC, KDKA, or KYW. Nowadays nobody knows or cares what station they have got as long as they can hear Bergen and McCarthy good and clear.

Oh, it was a wild modern world all right, and there was Barthelmess and his patent-leather hair, and the smart kids left their galoshes unbuckled.

Just to make our old burg perfectly typical we even had what my Uncle Elmo, who was a prop man around the old vaudeville circuits, used to call a "bughouse Hamlet." A bughouse Hamlet is an old boy who is all the time reciting Shakespeare. Our bughouse Hamlet was so small he could never have been mistaken for John Barrymore in any of the famous roles, and he wandered around town in an old ratty coat with a beaver collar on it surmounted by a derby hat of the old style with brims that curled up. He had been "on the stage," but on what stage and when nobody ever knew. The only stage he ever stood on in my lifetime was an empty Kingston cornstarch case, or a chair in Jake Stegelmeyer's speakeasy across from the courthouse.

"I suppose you think Warner Buckingham is a big joke," my Dad used to say. "Well, get one thing into your head, son, anybody who can reel off as much Shakespeare by heart as Warner can is no fool, even though he does sit around the midnight lunch counters."

"I never said he was a joke," I said.

"Everybody else does," said my Dad. "Don't get small-town like them. You have to look people over and find out what they really are; don't listen to what *anybody* in this town has to say."

I never actually took anything seriously that anybody in that old town had to say, but I must admit I listened. And I sure heard some swell stuff which I can't remember, but I wish I could because it was all for the birds and would prove in ten minutes that we might as well have pulled stakes and headed off for another county out further toward the setting sun. There was more assorted and unclassified varieties of ignorance running around loose in that town than you could find if you had a thousand years to make a door-to-door canvass of the whole world. I wouldn't say right out that my old town was the most ignorant in the U.S.A. because I have knocked around quite a bit and have hit some dumps that were pretty bad, but my old town was right up there in the semifinals for the title of Worst One-Peso Dump North of Key West, Fla.

Well, they say you shouldn't squawk about these things because people will think you are a sorehead and maybe left town by request of the authorities on account of being a firebug or a Mormon or having stole a screw driver from the hardware counter at Kresge's. I never did any of these things. I just went away. Some people go away and some people stay forever. Some of the people back there, lots of them, had never been to St. Paul, 90 miles away, and hadn't the slightest notion in the world of going, either. Then there was some who had been and said it didn't amount to much and the prices was away out of line and the restaurants a big gyp.

I was only a kid, but I must have felt it; I never had enough education to put in your eye in those god-damn public schools so it wasn't in quest of higher things that I left. It must of been that I just smelled a dead cat in the air, dumb as I was, and blew, because I wasn't unhappy at home, and at various times I even pictured myself in the pipe-and-slipper skit with Roma Schlesinger lighting the pipe.

I wonder where the hell Roma is now. She was a good queen. She was tall and had a real woman's shape even when I first met her at junior high school in the seventh grade. She was the smartest girl in class and if I must come out and admit it I was the smartest boy except in civics because I didn't care for Miss Kelly the teacher.

We used to go to parties and play Winkum and Post Office and write notes and she gave me her handkerchief and I gave her my skull-and-bones ring with glass eyes. Somebody got up a dancing class that we would have on Friday nights upstairs at the Eagles Hall. The music was piano and drum, and we only paid fifty cents apiece including Miss Schroeder the dancing teacher. After the dancing class we would walk up Main Street to Kassmeyer's Drugstore and sit in the booths making wisecracks and dipping into the chocolate-marshmallow sundaes and double malts with Nabisco Wafers. My Dad would be around and if they were short on fountain help, which they often were, he would help out. He was a great kidder and all the gang liked him.

About the time we started the dancing class in the fall of 1933 I got my first pair of long pants, blue corduroy.

"They're wonderful," Roma said. "Honestly I think you look just wonderful." I thought I looked wonderful too. Maybe I did, at that.

She used to let me kiss her and squeeze her and play around a little bit above the waist. When spring came the boundary line got lower and lower. So that was Roma and me for three or four years, before I pulled out to see the world. Since then I have had sixty-five girls including some old enough to be somebody's mother.

So Roma went out to North Dakota with her father the Professor and I went out wandering up and down the United States and the trains kept rumbling over the bridge from Wisconsin and blowing their whistles for the Third Street grade crossing, but neither of us was there any more to hear them or care whether they came or went or what kind of a season the high-school football team was having. I would sit on a timberhead or on the coaming of a coal barge going up the river in the evening listening to the Grease Cup and wondering what ever happened to Roma, who taught me how to make love and read poetry and who was way up ahead of me in brains.

Anyway I figured I had got about what I had coming to me. I could watch the world go by and hear it on the pilot-house radio and study my Correspondence Courses. All it cost me to live was a few pairs of work gloves and two pairs of shoes a year, and some whiskey and beer and hotel rooms, and a compact or silk stockings for some doll. The rest I put in the Boatmen's Bank of St. Louis and I had $9600 laying there, a pretty good stake.

But I wasn't going back to that old town I come from. Anyplace else, for sure.

Anyplace else, I'll guarantee that.

The Rajah is exploring the land ahead of the drifts and has been rewarded with good showing in the jack clippings.

—GALENA, ILL., *Herald*
December 24, 1908

10

THE Swede was right about the fog. We laid around drinking coffee most of the watch. Then I sent Swede down into the hole to clean up the lines and set Zero and Arkansaw to painting the walls in the deck hands' can, and I walked out over the tow in the dark two or three times and checked all the couplings and checked the running lights on the head barges. It was cooling off fast, like the Swede said, and when Ironhat would throw the searchlight upstream to pick up a buoy I could see fog patches on the water. Out on the barges it was cold and still, and all you could hear was the water gurgling between the loads. It was dark as could be and when Ironhat didn't have his light on

I used my flashlight to see where the hell I was going, especially at the couplings where the steel wires holding the barges together were grunting and squeaking with the strain.

About 4 A.M. Ironhat called me up to the pilothouse, and the fog patches were coming more frequent and thicker, and every once in a while we'd hit a fog blanket that would hide everything for a minute or so.

"I ain't taking any chances, Duke," Ironhat said. "We are going to tie this outfit up before it is so foggy we can't find no tree."

"It is not looking so good out there and I agree with you a hundred per cent," I said.

"We're about five mile below Clarksville Lock," he said, "and I figured I would get us up at least near the lock by watch time, but they ain't no use to flirting with fate."

"This fog could close down good any minute," I said. "And with the high water it would be a poor god-damn deal floundering around out here with ten thousand ton of coal."

"That's just what I know," he said, and added, "Them fools down in St. Louis."

"I'll get the yawl up on the head," I said. "Which side?"

"Port side," he said. "We are at Mulheron Field and I'll stick her in there. Plenty trees in there."

"O.K.," I said, and opened the door to go.

"Duke," Ironhat said.

"What?" I said.

"Put plenty line out."

"Two enough?"

"How about three?"

"We'll see how she hangs on two," I said. "Can you run your engines slow ahead and hold her up?"

"I suppose so. I wonder what they are doing in the big city tonight."

"They are all asleep," I said. "Everybody in the world is asleep except us."

"I believe you," Ironhat said and lit a new cigar. "The bastards are all asleep except us."

I went down the iron steps and rounded up the boys and lined it out for them. What we needed was two lock lines on the head of the barges, flashlights for everybody, and the yawl up there to row the lines onto the flooded island so as to make fast onto some good big elm or cottonwood tree. Ironhat could shove the barges in close, but drawing eight and a half feet as they were he couldn't get close enough for us to get to the trees without the yawl. We had a good long ladder out there too and that was a help sometimes.

"Get your god-damn life jackets on," I said. "And work slow and watch what the hell you are doing. I will beat hell out of the first one that drowns himself for the publicity."

I got a life jacket, and while Swede and Zero lowered the yawl off the roof into the river with the winch I slipped into the galley and grabbed a cup of coffee that was too hot and burnt my tongue.

Ironhat rung down for a half head and Kennedy give it to him. I went out and passed out flashlights and the boys begun to pull the yawl out ahead of the boat alongside the barges.

"Now don't for Christ sake fall in," I said.

"Ve don't fall in, Duke," said the Swede, like he was talking to some little kid.

"Come on you hillbilly," I said to Arkansaw. "You and me will carry out another lock line just in case."

"We already got two out there," he said. "How many you reckon we need?"

"Come on," I said. "Grab your half and shut up."

"My, my, how you talk," he said.

We got out on the head of the tow, eight hundred feet

from the boat or about a seventh of a mile away, and dumped
the line and Ironhat had his light on the shore but there
wasn't no shore, only water tearing down through the trees
on the island. Ironhat had one wonderful idea in tying her
off when he did—the fog was coming in fast and you couldn't
hardly see back to the boat.

"Cold as hell out here," says Arkansaw, and just then the
Swede and Zero showed up on the port side of the barge
dragging the yawl alongside.

"Listen," says Zero, "I think the pilot is hollering."

We shut up and from way back on the boat and across
the piled-up coal I heard Ironhat who had stuck the megaphone out the window.

"I can't see nothing back here," he squawked. "Where are
we at?" His voice sounded nine miles away.

"Run back quick like a race horse to the second coupling
and stand there and relay to Ironhat," I said, giving Arkansaw a shove. "Don't trip on nothing. Tell him we are a hunnerd feet from the trees and to let her fall in again the shore."

"Yeah man," Arkansaw said, setting off in the dark down
between the loads.

"As soon as we hit," I said to the Swede and Zero, "I'll
row, you Swede come with me and pay out line, and you
Zero stay here."

"Ve find good tree," the Swede said.

We all stood there and shined our flashlights on the deck
and laid out the lines. Ironhat had got the message and was
letting the whole works flop in toward the island. We could
see the trees through the misty fog and there was some good
ones. If we could get at them.

There was nothing to do for a minute, so we all lit up.
Thanks to the good Lord for tobacco. So we stood saying
nothing, feeling the damp and fog around us, and listening
to the water running down over the island. We couldn't hear

the engines even, back on the boat, but we heard a train a couple miles away over beyond the trees, coming down the west side below Clarksville, blowing for a grade crossing in a mournful way.

"One of these days I'm gonna take you up on that idea of deer hunting," I said to Swede. "You reckon I could get me a deer if I come up there to Two Harbors this fall?"

"You get deer. Deer all over. Ve go to Grand Marais. Plenty deer," he said.

"I wouldn't shoot no deer," Zero said.

"Vy not? Tam good eatin," says the Swede.

"I just wouldn't," Zero said.

"This is gonna drop in here fine I think," I said.

"Yo! Arkansaw!" I hollered back. "She's dropping in O.K. just like she is."

And then I heard him hollering back to Ironhat and Ironhat said something, but I couldn't make it out.

"You come up Two Harbors, Duke. Ve get good hunting. My brudder take us in car vay back in timber."

"I hope two lines will hold this old bitch," I said.

Pretty soon the barge began to bump and scrape bottom. We were right on top of the rock rip-rap I guess. The edge of the island was right underneath us.

"Yo! Arkansaw!" I hollered. "She's stopped. Hold her up right there!"

As I climbed down into the yawl I could hear him bellering at Ironhat and Ironhat bawling out something or other. The fog was coming in thick. Just in time. The Swede got in with me and I took the oars and pulled over into the trees while he payed out line. We got all fouled up in some limbs and my famous Mate's cap with the stars and all got knocked overboard and I nearly fell in grabbing it. I threw it onto the bottom of the yawl.

The current was really racing down over that island, and

in the dark and fog it was no place for a picnic with hot dogs and teasing the girls. Pretty soon I run into a cotton-wood tree that was a real granddaddy.

"Listen Swede," I says. "Pay out and I'll see if I can work us clear around her and back to the tow. Then we'll have one good double line on her anyways. Watch yourself now." A branch hit me in the eye and I cussed it good.

"We got enough line to run it back?" I said.

"Ve got plenty line yet, Duke."

By some freak or other in the atmosphere all of a sudden we could hear the pilothouse radio for a few seconds. Some old boy in a night club was blowing his brains out on a trumpet.

"I wish that bastard on the horn could change places with me for ten minutes," I said. "I'd give a tune by God."

I managed to squeeze the yawl to the upriver side of the tree and then she got stuck on a stump or something. After five minutes I got mad and slid over the side into the ice cold river and felt around with my feet. I got bottom and the water was up to my chest and I shoved the yawl free and bellied myself over the coaming into the yawl again, and we started clawing our way in the dark through the limbs and trash and drift logs back to the boat.

"Hey, the man wants to know what you guys are doin," Zero called to us.

"Tell him we are playin three-handed euchre with a mush-rat," I said. "And the rat is takin all the money."

"Ve get back to boat soon now," the Swede said. "Ve trow plenty hot coffee in you, Duke."

Pretty soon we got clear and got back to the barge and give Zero the line, and he took up as much slack as he could and made her fast to the timberheads, and we had one line on her anyway, doubled. So that was as good as two lines.

So we loaded another lock line into the yawl.

"I wisht I was in the island of Madagascar right now," I said.

Well we went through the same all over again only I didn't get into Old Man River again. I had had enough of that, and we got another double line around a pretty good size elm. A log went sailing by with a rabbit setting on it, crouched down with his ears laid back and more dead than alive. I tried to catch him but missed. By now the fog was so thick you couldn't see nothing.

"I bet he wonders what this is all about," I said.

Ironhat let the whole ten thousand tons drop back real easy and I checked one line against the other so as to have an equal strain on both and there we were and I went back through the fog and took off my pants and long underwear and my shoes and socks and stood in front of the galley stove naked and drunk a hundred cups of coffee and felt better. Clarence was there in his white clothes banging frying pans around. Ironhat came down himself for a look around.

"What the hell is this, a god-damn nudist colony?" he says.

"I was just in the romantic Mississippi up to my chin," I says. "There is nothing so refreshing on these hot nights as a good swim."

"Jesus was you in that water?" he said.

"The yawl got stuck and I had to get in and work her loose."

"Well," he says, "it's a gay life, ain't it?"

It was 5:30 by then and the messboy grabbed his bell and started off for his tour of the boat, ringing to beat hell.

So he died and she very imprudently married the barber.

11

TEN minutes later I was still standing there with a dish towel wrapped around me, waiting for the Swede to bring me down some dry clothes from my cabin and lo and behold in comes Jackoniski, the first time in the whole history of creation he ever got out of the sack without the benefit of dynamite, and although I didn't care if anybody else was around with me standing there bareass in front of the galley stove I didn't want my fellow Mate and bosom chum Jackoniski in the front row.

He come up to expectations and he says:

"Well, well, hello, Cupid."

I had had about enough of everything since I climbed out of that taxicab in St. Louis so I hit him and he went down fast and banged his head against the doorjamb and laid there looking mad and surprised. He never tried to get up and just laid there.

"Now what the hell is the idea of all this?" says Clarence, getting real incensed over the situation.

"That will teach you some manners maybe, you Chicago polecat," I says.

Jackoniski never said a word, he just come up to a sitting position and looked at me.

"You son of a bitch," he says finally.

"Never mind that," I says. "Go on in and eat your breakfast and discontinue the humorous remarks from now on."

"What in hell is the matter on this here boat?" says Clarence and just then back come Ironhat from the messroom where he had gone to get some sugar in his coffee.

"Now what?" he says. "What's the big god-damn idea staging a fight here in the galley?"

Behind Jackoniski the door opened and the Swede come in with my dry clothes and fell over Jackoniski and lit on the floor. Jackoniski gave him a kick and says, "Get off me you ——in dumb Swede."

Well the Swede didn't mind being called the Swede all the time except when somebody called him the *dumb* Swede, which is standard with Swedes; so he got mad and give pal Jackoniski a kick right back, as good as he could being sprawled on the floor and mixed up with my clothes.

"I dumb Svede you, by golly," he says and give the heroic Pole another kick with his wet boot, but he missed.

"What the hell is going on in here on my boat?" says Casey, coming on watch in a quick hurry and roaring like four bulls as he come into the galley from the messroom. "A god-damn flood all around us and all you boys got to do is get up a fight."

The Swede got up and picked up my clothes and gave

them to me and went out the door into the greasy old fog.

Jackoniski got up and went out without his breakfast.

Casey went in and sat down at the head of the table and the messboy looking all fussed up took him in his coffee.

I put on my clothes and went out to see what the boys were doing because we were all still on watch for another ten minutes, and there is Jackoniski standing by the engine-room door.

"We'll finish this up some other time," I says. "Right now we got to get the coal up the river."

"This boat ain't big enough to hold you and me," he says.

"All right," I says. "If anybody goes it ain't going to be me. You can get off up at the lock. I'll take this bitch clear to Hudson's Bay on double watch."

"I spose you think I'm gonna quit," he says. "You'd like that, wouldn't you though?"

"Any time. Right now," I says.

"You and your ——in correspondence courses," he says.

"Yeah what about 'em?" I says.

"You think you're better than everybody else, don't you?"

"Yeah, a lot better."

"Well maybe I ain't gettin off."

So I went up forward and Arkansaw was coiling down a line and the Swede leaning against the capstan in the bright light of the deck lights. They didn't say anything and I lit a cigarette and walked out on the tow to check the shore lines. As I walked out in the pea soup I wondered whether I had done wrong or not, and whether it is a good idea to drive a rat off the boat or let him stay and run loose. I could give Swede the other watch when I was tired, if Jackoniski got off, but I figured the lousy bum would stay on.

"What was the idea in that?" Casey said to me later, when I went up to the pilothouse before going to bed. We were still tied off in the fog, of course, and the only sound was the generator blamming away up in the forward end of the engine room. All you could see was the fog swirling around —you couldn't see six feet, and it was damp and cold and a lot of static on the radio.

"You ain't been living in the same room with that lazy squint all these months like I have," I said, but I was sore at myself and feeling bad about it too.

"If you wanted to hit him why in hell did you decide on the galley? That don't look good. What's the matter with you anyways, Duke, are you getting jumpy or something?"

"No, I ain't getting jumpy."

"You sure act it."

"No, I don't neither."

"The hell you don't."

"Well, I ain't."

"Maybe not, but you sure ain't yourself."

"How ain't I myself for the Christ sake? Who tied this damn mess off last night? *Me. I'm* all right. Just don't bother your head about *me. I'll* make it. *I'll* be here," I said.

"Is Jackoniski staying?"

"I don't know," I said. "If he isn't I will gladly stand all the Mates' watches on this boat by my individual self for three years just so long as I don't have to look at the dregs of Poland no more."

"Oh he ain't that bad," says the Captain.

"He is three times that bad in spades," I said. "He ain't washed his socks in four months for one thing."

"Oh go way."

"I am deathly afeared he'll change his mind about getting off is all," I said. "I'll bet by the time we get out of this fog and up to that lock he'll decide to stay. Casey, do me a favor some sweet day and fire that bum, will you? I could make a Second Mate out of anybody, even the messboy or the Kid, who would do as good as him."

"What's the matter with you? I know Jackoniski is no rose but we been putting up with him all these months."

"Well his time has run out as far as I'm concerned."

"Yeah well it just so happens I am still running this boat. Maybe you better lay down and cool off," he says like a big Captain.

Instead of hitting him with the leg of a chair I went out without saying another word. I always liked Casey all right— he kept a clean boat and never held the grocery order down like some and he was always a pleasure to work with up till he started playing the big rough tough sea captain with me. I got halfway down the stairs and then came back and opened the door and stuck my head in.

"Good night, *Captain*," I said, and went down the stairs and felt better for I could hear him stomping around and cussing.

I bet Jackoniski would decide to stay. He knew a good thing when he had it and he really had it right there on that boat, including swiping my cigarettes and loafing all through the evening watch. He had been pulling all this stuff for years and getting away with it, which just shows what a grand and glorious country of opportunity for hamburgerheads we got to grow up in here. On top of it all we now had on our hands the uplifting sight and sound of Casey the mighty Captain sticking up for this escapee from a garbage dump and taking sides with him against Me, his Mate and Faithful Pal through thick and thin, mostly thin, when it wasn't thick.

Long days and long nights on the river, a couple of centuries in boxcars and looking at the cold stars from alleys where you go to piss or throw up, a hundred light-years of reading about the politicians in the newspapers as the leaves drop and the sleet begins to cover the sidewalks and tarpaper shanties, all of eternity with a free lunch thrown in and you will never find out anything definite on anybody.

They are all slippery as Mississippi mud. All the brains dis-
played in my Correspondence Courses put together can't
seem to improve the natural orneriness of the human race
or predict where the hell it is going to break out next. Somebody or other invented soap so we can all keep clean, but
nobody thought up nothing yet to clean up the insides of
people's heads, and the way things look, especially in the
taverns around midnight, why the human race is getting
dirtier every day.

So I went down to my cabin pretty mad and climbed into
the sack and read a lesson in my Correspondence Course on
American history, but I didn't find a thing in there to cheer
me up—it was the same selection of bums we have today,
only they wore funny clothes and had never heard of bub-
ble gum.

So I turned out the light and layed there thinking it over
and wondering when the fog would lift and whether Jackoniski would stay or go, and cussing his family for ever leaving
Warsaw and jumping into the melting pot of the great Republic. Then I wondered if I was really getting jumpy like Casey
said, or whether it was him. Then I got indigestion, but I
was too lazy to get up and take some Pepto-Bismol, so finally
I fell asleep and we were still fogged in someplace below
Clarksville, Missouri, while the earth went on spinning
around and around.

That's the way it is when we get depressed thinking of
our misspent life, and we imagine that we should take some
nice girl up in front of the congregation and get married and
settle down in a cement-block house with a sun porch and
two unfinished rooms on the second floor. Guess who is going
to finish those two rooms on Saturday afternoons and week-
day evenings? That's right.

"By God if I was married I would sure get off these here
boats," I used to tell the Grease Cup.

"Maybe you would and maybe you wouldn't," he would say. "That remains to be seen."

"It don't remain nowhere because I ain't *about* to get married," I always said.

We had a neighbor at home he was a fireman and then later on an engineer on the Milwaukee road, and he spent a lifetime making a showplace out of his house and lot. He had *two* range boilers made into flower boxes in the front yard. Whenever he went on his vacation he brought back stones or seashells or pieces of petrified wood and then he built a fountain out of all of the pieces. He spent God knows how long building a rock garden with a rock from every State in the Union in it, and the American flag made out of different-colored pieces of bathroom tile. Then he made a lily pool with bottle caps set into the concrete all around the edge. He must have put in thirty years in his spare time on the whole layout and finally got a feature story about him and his yard in the Sunday paper. Well he got so fired up over this that he begin to overreach himself and laid the foundations for a genuine Dutch windmill, which was to be about thirty feet high with colored lights on the vanes. He got it halfway done in between calls to pull freight trains, and had bought a two-horse motor to turn the windmill and figured he would maybe make the *Minneapolis Tribune* this time, when all of a sudden he died, and the property went to his son-in-law who sold it to a barber from down-river at New Albin who got a bulldozer in and knocked the whole works down and put in sixty-five peony plants and threw the range boilers on the city dump.

Which shows that fame does not last very long and brings up the query as to whether it is worth while to settle down or not.

Of course this engineer had a lot of fun and he thought he was going to go down in history alongside of Alexander

Graham Bell, or Burbank. He never once suspected all his good works were going to be wiped out by a barber less than thirty days after he got settled down in the casket for a long winter's nap.

I used to stand out on the barges in the evening, after I gave up roaming throughout the Great Western Plains area and became a sober, righteous, and God-fearing Steamboat Man, and look across the river and into the trees and through the scraggly little islands and wonder a lot of things about life, liberty, and the pursuit of a living wage, but there was never an answer in the sunset and I would return and lie down in my bunk among the other deck hands as they lay snoring their guts out in expectation of the next call on deck.

Now Father was always about to give up the truss-fitting vocation and go out West and raise sheep, but he never got there because his house burnt up one night due to mice or faulty wiring, and he never got to the thirty-second degree of the Masonic Lodge as he had planned, so the mice won that round. Father would never have gone anyway. By that time he was too old to uproot and go anyplace else, even twelve miles away from that intellectual garbage dump called my home town by the mystic Father of Waters.

Kassmeyer's nephew, a "sallow youth" with stringy hair and a cheap suit, came into the business and inherited the whole shooting gallery anyway, including the right to pinch the soda-fountain girls and take them home from work once in a while. He was a bottle of imitation lemon soda all right, but by now he is on a Committee and everybody says "Hello" to him. And he still hasn't combed his hair yet.

So I slept on in the fog, tied up to two trees below Clarksville, Missouri, and the flood ran down over the islands on both sides. Somewhere down-river below us that rabbit was still riding on his log, and it was a question whether he would pull through the flood or die.

*Troublesome problems seemed to be multiply-
ing for Tom Swift.*

—TOM SWIFT AND HIS PHOTO TELEPHONE

12

To this day I believe Jackoniski went out in the fog
that morning and sunk that barge. I don't see any other way
or means that barge would have gone down. And it sure
went down.

I went off watch at 6 A.M. and Jackoniski went on. The fog
hung on until 10 A.M. before you could see half a barge
length. And then old One Eye went out with the Kid to
check up and when they got there the barge on the port
side was sunk and a thousand tons of coal with it and just
by chance the whole damn tow was hanging there by one of
the coupling wires that had, by some miracle or other, not
broke. Well of course there was one hell of an uproar, but

what was there to do about it? Casey called Chicago Marine and talked to the office on the ship-to-shore and all that anybody could figure out was to leave her there until the flood was over. No salvage crew would come up there from St. Louis right then anyway. So the insurance company and the other brains finally come to the same decision we had come to in the first place, namely, "Leave her lay there."

This barge that went down was famous already among us Mates and deck hands, who have to know every barge as though we had spent the night in a double bed with it in the Mark Twain Hotel. This was an old bitch who had been bunged and banged and slammed around since 1925 on every river except the Sacramento, and had been sunk and raised again four times, had hit the lock wall at Louisville and opened a hole big enough to drive a Chevrolet into, had so many welds and patches on her rakes and knuckles you couldn't tell just what was original and what had been pieced on in different shipyards. She also had a sea cock in her for some reason known only to the architect who laid her out on the board.

What I figured was this fine all-American boy Jackoniski went out there in the fog some time between 6 A.M. and 7 A.M. and opened the sea cock. All he would have to do was go down the manhole on the port side and open her up. She had a gate valve.

You see nobody would pay much attention to that, if and when they ever raised the barge. And with the stage of water, why by the time they got it up Jackoniski could be most anyplace, far away if necessary. And the barge would be a mess and probably wracked and twisted, and by that time only the salvage crew would be there and the company wouldn't know or care anything as long as they got their insurance or their barge back and reimbursed for the coal, which would have to be removed before raising.

Jackoniski thought I would get the blame for tying up wrong, on top of rocks, or not checking the barge for leaks, or something. He had it doped out that I would get sent to Siberia or Boys' Town and have my Mate's License revoked and he would get the Mate's job while I was hauled away with the bracelets on by a dick in a derby hat.

All that happened instead was a hell of a lot of trouble and the usual accident reports to fill out and there would have been a Coast Guard hearing on it before the Inspectors of the St. Louis District, I suppose, only something else happened which gave the Inspectors something more important to ask questions about.

"Listen, Duke, did you sound that barge after we tied off there?" Casey asked me when they had got me out of bed again after a fine relaxing three hours of sleep.

"Hell no, I didn't. I come in to dry off after being in the river," I said. "Anyway it was 5:30 A.M. by that time and by the time I got into some dry clothes . . ."

"And staging a prize fight in the galley."

"Yeah, yeah. And by the time I got dressed, why man it was 6 o'clock already and I was off watch."

"Well they are gonna climb on me over this," Casey said.

That don't hurt my feelings none, I thought.

So old number 36, a barge that had kissed every lock wall in the inland waters and been aground or sunk in every navigable river west of Morgantown in her twenty-five years of life, was sunk and sunk good. The bank where we were tied to ran off fast into deep water, and there was six feet of nice cold spring flood water running over her decks.

Later in the day there was more hell over the short-wave radio and Casey gradually got more sore at me the more insults he got from the office via radio. He didn't come right out and say so but he told Ironhat that barge must have had water in it all during our watch or how in hell could it have sunk so fast?

"Did you tell Jackoniski to sound the barges when you went off watch?" he said.

"Hell no," I said. "He knows that's the very first thing we do each and every morning. Christ I don't have to tell him that. *You* was on watch with him. Did *you* tell him? What was he doing anyway?"

How would the great Captain Casey know what Jackoniski was doing that morning? As soon as Ironhat and I went to bed Casey told One Eye to call him when the fog lifted and then laid down on the pilothouse bench for a nap. I never let on I knew that, but I had asked One Eye and that's what he told me.

"What the hell was Jackoniski doing?" I asked One Eye.

"I seen him go out on the tow," says One Eye, "and then I never seen him for quite a while. The Kid and Stevie was down in the hole suppose to be repairing lines."

"Didn't nobody sound the tow to see if any of the goddamn barges was taking water?"

"I guess we figured it was different from other mornings on account of the fog. I guess we figured we'd sound after we got turned loose and was going up the river."

"What the hell was *you* doing all this time?"

"Setting up in the lonesome pilothouse in the pilot's chair, watching for the fog to lift and listening to Casey snore."

"One Eye, what do you reckon made that barge decide to sink all of a sudden with four thousand dollars' worth of coal in her?"

"You reckon they will have an investigation by the Inspectors?"

"Yeah. But what made her sink?"

"How much that barge worth?"

"Well, she's old and beat up, but still worth fifteen or

twenty thousand dollars, I guess. A new one costs forty thousand now, so they say. Listen, One Eye, what made her sink so sudden?"

"Search me. Maybe when we touched bottom when we tied up she knocked one of them patches off her bottom, or opened up a weld. Is that rock bottom?"

"Yeah. We're on riprap. But hell, we grounded as light as a feather. We didn't have no headway. She more or less floated in until she hit bottom and stopped."

"Them god-damn fools in the office. Now just imagine if you was a poor boy to begin with, and had worked and slaved to get to the point eventually where you was the owner of a towboat and a fleet of barges. Now let's just say you was them owners, O.K.?"

"O.K."

"All right. Here's the ——in picture: the whole Upper Mississippi has gone nuts with water from the Minneapolis coal docks clear to Cayro. And it is still rainin up North. The ——in river is up so high it is over the railroad tracks. Now what would you do if you was the owner?"

"I am not likely to be an owner of a barge fleet, so don't rush me," I says.

"Well, would you put eight ——in loads in front of your ——in towboat, which is a good enough shover through the summer months, but no ——in champ any time and much less on a ——in flood stage of water? Would you do that?" One Eye said, spitting.

"No, I reckon I wouldn't do that," I said.

"Them fools down in St. Louis," he said, glaring at me with his good eye. "Next trip they will probably send us across the ——in Pacific Ocean to Bordoo, France, or Argentinia or some such place."

Casey was still up in the brain box talking to the Chicago office over the short wave, and having a poor time of it.

"What made her sink, Clarence?" I queried quietly, entering the galley where our good old unperturbed cook was laying up some slab cakes for supper.

"Them mushrats and beavers got mad of the invasion of their privacy," says Clarence, "and chewed a hole in her."

"I wish to hell Casey would get done jawing with the big brains and we would get under way," I said.

"Number 36 she is going to be down there for a while," he said.

"You know she is," I said. "She is going to be down there for just a fine long time."

"In fact we might never see her again," he said, and dumped five drops of red coloring into the cake frosting.

"What happened to that barge anyway?" I said to Ironhat, who couldn't sleep and came wandering into the galley looking pale behind his cigar stub.

"The son of a bitch done sunk like many a barge has done before," he said. "They have been sinking since George Washington's time. And she sunk on the other watch, Duke. They are trying to pin some sweet ——in 'negligence' on you and me, but she never sunk until *four hours* or thereabouts after you and me tied off and went off watch. What was the other watch doing for four hours they never noticed old number 36 was going down? Tell me that, Mister Mate, tell me a real quick answer to that?"

"Maybe the Inspectors will think to ask that question too," I said. "By God I hope so."

"You may remember," he said, applying a match to his old wet cigar stub, "that on that romantic night when we left Alton, Illinois, with eight loads I said to you, I said, 'Them fools down setting there in the office at St. Louis they don't know what they are doing sending us up here onto a flood stage.' The fools are thinking of them big rivals, River Transit. They are worrying about their loan at the bank.

They none of them have ever been out here on the river so they don't know, but this time they are going to get it right where the old gray goose got it on Christmas Eve."

"Oh hell, we was shoving slow, but at least coming up the river until this old barge decided to take a swim," I said. "We wasn't setting no speed records I'll admit plainly. But that goddam number 36. I'll swear she was O.K. when I left her at 5:30 a.m."

"Tell it to the ——in board of ——in directors," he said.

"I don't know them too good," I said, "or I would. I don't hardly ever get invited to no parties at their house."

"I think it was all Clarence's fault," Ironhat said, ashing his butt into the sink. "Why in the hell don't you come clean and admit you done it, Clarence?"

"Very funny," Clarence said. "Would you mind just moving over onto the other side of the room and giving me a little space? Better still why don't you two radio comics move into the messroom and finish the ——in discussion in there?"

"I am going up and lay down," Ironhat said, and he did.

I went out and looked at the river and it was cold and gray and the fog had lifted for a while but settled down into a cold drizzle, so the islands over across the way looked hazy and pale. The decks were wet and had a dull shine to them and the river smell was strong. Unless you have ever smelled the Mississippi River you don't know what that means and no use to attempt an explanation, but she smells like islands and willows and railroad ties and mud and she smells like Minnesota and Illinois and Wisconsin and Iowa and parts of Missouri, all mixed up together. Then she smells like standing under a bridge, or sitting in a duck blind, and like old overalls and marine engines, and like a retriever when he is crouched shivering in the boat on the way home. She also smells like wet oilskins, coal smoke, dead catfish and buffalo and gar pike, like rotten logs and hepaticas on the hillsides, and like the whiskey breath of an old deck hand who can't quite remember where he come from.

"What made her sink is what I want to know," I said to Mr. Kennedy, the bilious engineer on our watch. "They are trying to pin it on us naturally. But what caused her to sink? What in hell was the cause of that anyways?"

"I don't know nothing about barges, thank god, and don't care to, neither," he said. "If I would of been interested in barges I wouldn't of gone into the engine room to begin with. All I want to know is when we going to leave this sunk barge here and get on up the river. I got a date in the Marine Hospital in St. Louis in ten days and the way we are going why we'll never get to Twin Cities before ice comes in."

Wasn't he right, though.

"What's this hospital deal?" I said. "How come you going into Marine Hospital?"

"I am just merely going to have one half of my stomach removed is all," he said. "And unless I do why I am a dead mallard."

"What! They going to cut out half your stomach?"

"Now just keep all that to yourself, Mate, will you? Just forget about that."

"But say, that's quite an operation ain't it?" I said.

"I didn't have it yet," he said. "How would I know?"

There was no sense in laying there tied up in the flood for seven years waiting for the big shots to tell us what to do. Number 36 was beyond anything we could do for her, and the best and only money-making policy was to get on up the river—if you could call it a river any more when she was over her banks and running down Main Street—and deliver the coal and get on back down to Alton for more of the same.

"Well, Kid, you are getting a swell slice of life on the Mississippi," I said to the boy who put the coal into the wrong cellar. "How would you like to be right back there at home now? You could go over there to the hotel where your brother is bellhop and read the magazines at the news stand and go through two or three Baby Ruth bars."

"I am gettin along all right here," he said. "I don't care to be down there at the hotel. Gee, they won't let nobody read them magazines without you are gonna buy one."

"Where was you when the barge went down?" I said. I was sure worried about that barge.

"I was downstairs in the bottom of the boat cleanin up and settin around."

"What was your Mate doing all the time?"

"I never seen him. I can't rightly say where he was at."

"Why did that barge dive, Kid? Why did that goddam old number 36 decide to sink on us?"

"Well, I'll tell you," says the Kid, taking out a stick of Beeman's Pepsin Gum, "I've got a theory about that."

"I'll bet it's a killer," I said. "So go ahead, pride of Alton, Illinois, and tell us the theory."

"Well," says the Kid, going to work on the gum with artistic jaw motions like the dime-store clerks back in 1933, "the way I see it is like this here: the barges sure they float despite of the fact they are made of steel and filled with coal, which proves the law of gravity, but on the other hand when we landed there on the shore it seems like we might of hit some rocks or somethin."

"Why, we drifted in there easy," I said. "We no more than merely nudged that riprap."

"Well to make a long story short my theory is like this: I figure the river was to blame. I think some water got in that barge somehow and she sunk."

"How much did you make," I says, "when you was helping on that coal truck down at Alton?"

"Niney-five cents an hour," he said.

"Well I hope you didn't give them no theories on the origins of coal," I said. "For god's sake go and disappear someplace will you?" I was peeved for the first time in the world at the Kid with all his razor-sliced baloney, for once it didn't seem funny, showing conclusively what a poor shape I was in.

But the Kid was right about one thing anyway, the barge sank because some water got into it. There is practically no other reason a barge will sink unless it gets some water into the insides.

The truth of the matter is that by the time a barge has been around as long as old number 36, it develops a suicide complex. It gets so tired of being banged into lock walls, thumped against pile clusters and piers and cobblestone levees and limestone riprap, sunk and raised again, run aground and yanked off, frozen by the ice water up the Illinois in January and boiled during the summer months down around Baton Rouge, tortured by welders and pneumatic chipping hammers and a feets of crude coarse deck hands tromping up and down on her decks, and generally pushed, shoved, banged around and made sport of and despised and looked down on by the younger barges as it grows older that it comes finally to the conclusion nothing would be quite so sweet as oblivion. There is a moral there for the congregation if any members care to seek it out. My private theory is, in spite of my suspicions of Jackoniski and possible dirty work in that department, that the poor old barge just plain got tired of life, issued the statement "Farewell cruel world" into the fog, and sank beneath the cold unfriendly flood waters of the Upper Mississippi just to get away from it all.

You really can't blame number 36 too much.

*Old Doc Noonan, who meets all trains, is being
missed down at the depot.*

—J. P. MC EVOY

13

So we started on up the mighty Mississippi after
four thousand conversations via Radio-Marine through
Chicago to the St. Louis office, where the Vice President in
charge of traffic suggested all sorts of wonderful alterna-
tives over the ether waves such as raising the barge with the
two-horsepower portable bilge pump, raising the barge by
having deck hands dive with saucepans and bring out lumps
of coal three at a time, and other schemes known only to
marine superintendents who spend their time studying the
channel out at the Country Club with the big problem being
the dog-leg hole. I use to be a caddy for one real swell summer up there in my famous home town and do I know these

captains of industry inside out? Well just go into the caddy business for one short month and you will know what makes them big bank accounts.

So we left old number 36 laying there under the flood with one timberhead sticking out and she was a pathetic sight as we left about 2 P.M., but not one half as pathetic as the face on Casey, who had received some good sharp remarks from the home office over the ship-to-shore and whereas Negligence and Incompetence were not actually mentioned in so many words they were there for all to read between the air waves.

So we left upriver and was Casey ever fit to be tied and sent to the slaughterhouse? Boy he was really pissed off at himself and at everybody aboard including the messboy, who was not involved in the sinking at all of barge number 36.

We dragged on up the river and she was really coming down at us now. Over by the railroad tracks when we come over to the Missouri side was a work train with three flatcars covered with sandbags, and a gang who would never have been admitted to Kincaid County, Illinois, after 6 P.M. were picking those heavy sandbags up and dumping them alongside the tracks. The water was already up to the ties and when the colored boys dropped a sandbag off their shoulders they would jump back and a big splash would go up. And then the next boy would flip a sandbag off his shoulder. Meanwhile the fireman leaned out of the cab picking his teeth disdainfully and looking at the steamboat go by. There was a little plume of steam off the whistle that broke and faded away against the brown of the hillside behind the engine.

The sky was gray in the east and blue in the west and the wind was from the east, so we never had the sun at all that day and number 36 lay back there under water at Mulheron Field, badly sunk.

We got up to Clarksville Lock finally and locked through and the lock tenders said we had a lot of guts to come on up in there with seven loads. They didn't say that to Ironhat, but they said it to me as I was standing out there in the coal barges.

"You guys ain't just exactly playing it smart up here in this flood with seven loads," says Ratface, a former deck hand of mine now retired to the glories of lock tending.

"Well, Ratface," I said. "We did not exactly start off with seven on purpose. If you want some free coal, hop in somebody's john boat and go on down to Mulheron Field because we left nearly a thousand ton down there and it is only a few feet under water. That is why we are all lobsided here with seven."

"No thanks," he said. "On this high water I am staying right up here where I am. But that is a shame about the barge."

"Ain't it though?" I said. "Listen, what report have you got from above? Is she on a crest yet?"

"Crest? Crest? Why, Duke, ain't you got no radio there? This is just beginning. She is going to go to twenty-three feet up at Dubuque, they say. Why these locks will all be shut down in a few days, I bet."

"Swell, Ratface, that's fine," I said.

Casey went up to the lock house and called St. Louis on the phone again and then we heard that the office was sending a salvage crew up to get number 36, but by that time number 36 was more or less of a dead issue to us; it was twelve miles behind us and already forgotten by everybody except me and Casey.

"Keep them deck hands out of my icebox at night or I'm gettin off at Quincy and you boys can heat up canned beans from there on into St. Paul," Clarence said to me when I entered the galley after we locked through and were creeping up the greasy old river again in a new drizzle.

"Can't you keep them deck hands from getting into the icebox at night?" Casey says to me. "What the hell, is this boat going nuts?"

"The cook is blaming me," says the messboy, coming into my cabin while I am setting on the edge of my bunk thinking it all over and smoking a cigarette and having a moment's peace and reflection to myself, "because the deck hands have been into the icebox on the night watches. It ain't my fault, I . . ."

"Get out," I said.

"Duke," says the Grease Cup, "this thing about the deck hands getting into the ice chest at night. You know that don't go on the boats. You got to nip that in the bud, boy. These here deck hands they will simply take over the whole boat you let them get away with that kind of thing."

"Grease Cup," I said, but he saw I was mad and he said, "All right, forget I ever said anything about it."

"How are them engines?" I said. "How is that steering rig holding up?"

"You are beginning to talk like big Casey the mighty Captain," he said.

"Now, don't let's you and *me*, for gawd's sake, have a fight," I said. "I am having enough fights here for the Madison Square Garden in New York City."

"I am sorry, Duke," the Grease Cup said with his big kindly simple face. "This is the god-damnedest poorest excuse for a trip up the river I ever seen is all."

"I'll raise you a dollar on that one," I said. "I'll bet it's one of the poorest trips anybody ever made. We are sure giving a poor impression of them fun-loving rivermen the papers write up."

"Let's go and drownd our sorrows in a cup of coffee," the Grease Cup said.

We walked down the guard and went into the galley. Clarence was taking his afternoon siesta and there was nobody there except the coffeepot, rattling and talking to itself on the back of the stove. The Cup poured out a sample into a clean mug, but after tasting it he threw it down the sink and began to make a new pot while I reached for a toothpick on the bottom shelf next to the cream of tartar.

"That boy Ratface down there at the lock says this little old flood is just getting started," I said looking out through the ventilating fan at the sky. "He says the locks are going to shut down. He says it is going to twenty-three feet at Dubuque. He says we must be nuts. He says . . ."

"Oh hell what is the difference anyway," the Grease Cup said. "My God I wish Clarence would lay off this brand of coffee," he said, measuring out. "For the same price he could get some real coffee. This here coffee, why we are just paying an advertising bill of a couple million a year for them to advertise the coffee and the product is no good. That's so damn typical of Clarence—and Casey too for that matter—for of course Clarence is buying this junk to please Casey; in fact Casey he thinks this coffee is just wonderful—he says, 'My that's a good cup of coffee. Ain't that a real cup of coffee for a change?' I come pretty near to blowing a fuse, but I says, 'Yes, that is some cup of coffee all right.' That is another clear-cut example of the ignorance of some of your mighty steamboat captains. They think they know coffee . . ."

"Well," I said, "if it goes to twenty-three feet at Dubuque we will be lucky if we can even find a place to tie up. By God I am glad *again*, Grease Cup, that I am the stupid type that don't want to be a pilot."

It was warm and it smelled good in the galley and for once

there was nobody in there elbowing you out of the way or boring you to death. There was just me and the Grease Cup and it was midafternoon, a quiet time on a steamboat usually. Outside, well, there it was all around us—cold water— and over on the islands more cold water trying to knock the trees and shanties down. But in the galley it smelled good, and like I said it was warm and dry and not the way it was outside where it was cold and *damp*, by God, like only the river valley can be in the spring.

When the coffee was done we took our cups into the messroom and sat down at the table with the red and white checkered tablecloth. I got up and took a handful of cookies out of one of the cookie boxes and picked up a couple of apples and sat down again and gave the Cup an apple.

"What difference anyway?" he said. "Suppose it goes to twenty-three feet, what then? We can find someplace to tie off. Then we will set there on top of the flood drinking this famous brand of Casey's favorite coffee. What's the difference as long as we are on the payroll?"

"How about your old lady? She is going to have six fits when she starts reading the papers. Listen, Bolts and Nuts," I said, "I don't think your mammoth brain has grasped the idea here yet."

"Never mind the old lady, she won't worry none. Milly she is past all that, you know," he said, taking out his pearl-handled pocketknife and beginning to peel his apple scientifically. "But what didn't my mammouth brain get ahold of? What do you mean by that?"

"Why you god-damn grease monkey do you reelize we are already above the flood stage of 1939? What we are doing out here at all is one for Ignatz to answer."

"Oh you boys on deck are always in a sweat about something," he said. "You know I put an egg in this here coffee. It tastes some better, don't it?"

"Why don't you get rid of that woman of yours if you are
so much smarter than us fools on deck?" I said. "By god I
would unload if I was you and that is for certain sure."

"No you wouldn't, Duke, not if I told you the whole story
sometime. I am stuck with Milly for good and all and there
ain't a blessed thing in the world anybody can do about it."

"Well," I said, "go ahead and tell me about it. It will get
my mind off this swell mess we are in up here."

The Grease Cup kept working on his apple, peeling it very
slow and careful and not looking at me.

"Well, Duke, I guess I never told you, but once upon a
time, about ten years ago when Milly and me was first married why we had a kid. But the kid died when he was about
a week old."

I begun to wish I had never brought up the subject, but it
was too late now.

"After the baby died why it seems she couldn't have no
more kids. She took it hard. Milly loved kids and she knew
I wanted kids. We had done a lot of god-damn foolish talk
about what we would make of him if he was a boy, like a
lawyer or a doctor and all that. And I remember I said if it
was a girl I wanted her to have pigtails and Milly she
laughed and said that was too old-fashioned. So she took it
hard. And of course it was up to me to pretend like I didn't
care. We had a bad time. I use to wake up at night sometimes and hear her bawling. Then she got so as she couldn't
go through with the bed performance no more. We ain't
been real man and wife for ten years now. Well I don't know
what the hell I am tellin you all this crap for," the Grease
Cup said and hauled out his blue bandana and blew his
nose with a snort.

"Go ahead," I said. "Spill it. You might feel better."

"There ain't no more to it," he said. "Except one funny
thing. Before she lost the baby why she never cared a bit

about the moving-picture shows. Oh we would go once in a while, you know, but oh like once or twice a month. Well a while after the baby she begun to go to the shows until it got so bad she was going every day and sometimes both the matinee and the evening performance. It's ten years now and she is still at it, like you know. Funny thing, ain't it?"

"Yeah," I said. "Well, she's probly . . ."

"The way I look at it the shock about the baby give her a screw loose someplace. She ain't never been the same. And then this game about the movies. That ain't natural."

"Well you wanna thank God she never took to the drink from it anyways," I said. "Or to setting in bars and running around."

"So you see, Duke, there ain't no use in your sayin I should unload Milly. She ain't hardly no wife to me at all, but at the same time, why damn it I can't run off and leave her. Can I now?"

"I don't know, George," I said, for that was the Cup's real name. I hardly ever called him that. "The Almighty is sure working overtime though, as usual, to see that everybody is happy."

"Yeah. Well, that's life I guess," he says.

"I never realized you had no problem like that," I said. "I guess I ain't going to kid you no more about the old lady all the time going to the picture shows."

"Oh that's all right," he said, cutting his apple up into neat little sections and spearing them and eating them off the end of his knife. "That don't bother me none any more."

"That's a tough deal, George," I said. What in the world was there to say anyway?

"It ain't no picnic," he said.

He went into the galley and got the pot and we had another cup of coffee.

"I don't know what I unloaded all that onto you for," he

said. I could have agreed with him 100 per cent only I was too polite.

"That's all right, George," I said.

"That is just between you and me, Duke."

"Yeah that is just between you and me, I would never have no occasion to get on that subject anyway with anybody else," I said. God forbid.

"I know that," he said eating the last piece of apple; and then we sat there listening to the rumble of the big screws under us down under the water and feeling the towboat shake and tremble and try to rattle herself apart.

So the Grease Cup had his Milly and Kennedy had his stomach about to be removed and the Kid's old man had run off and left them all behind to look out for themselves; Casey was in bad with the company on account of sinking number 36 and Ironhat was scared to death over the flood and I had punched Jackoniski and knocked him onto the galley floor; and upriver there was more water coming down at us than anybody had ever seen before since steamboats began. The only calm ones aboard was Zero because he was too dumb to know any better and the Swede because he was used to worse things and born calm anyway. There is very little on the watery part of the world that will scare a Swede.

So I went out on the tow and sat on a timberhead so far away from the boat that I nearly forgot about it, and I tried to think things out, but I am a very poor thinker and practically nothing come of it.

Well, we had our troubles again that night, nothing serious but we had to tie up and by noon the next day we had got noplace and were still below Hannibal floundering around and making no money at all. But we finally got up to Saverton Lock late in the afternoon and locked on through. And when we had locked through Saverton Lock the news spread

through the boat like tear gas that we were going to tie up at
Hannibal while the engineers performed some mysterious
actions on the engines or the pumps or the steering or something.

"Where in the hell we will tie up is a nice question," says
Clarence. "The god-damn levee must be clear under. It is
over the railroad tracks I imagine."

But we got her tied up, below the highway bridge, and
there was strict orders that nobody was to leave the boat
under any pretext or other whatsoever. Everybody was to
stay aboard and no trips uptown to the taverns or after newspapers and cigarettes and copies of girlie magazines and
those half pints of whiskey that used to turn up empty out in
the coal piles sometimes after a tie-up. So naturally everybody immediately began to plot and plan ways to get uptown. It was 8 P.M. and it was now pouring rain again, but
that never yet stopped a steamboat man who wanted to go
uptown and here we were right in old Mark Twain's front
yard, and the taverns just a few hundred yards away still
had the lights on and the bottles lined up on the back bar
glittering like the crown jewels of Imperial Russia. There
were sidewalks to walk on, and fire-engine houses, and voices
to listen to for a few minutes that were different from all the
voices on the boat. There might even be girls to look at in
the taverns, with rings on their fingers and bracelets on their
fat greasy wrists. They would laugh, giggle, sit silently, or
act like fools—no matter. And no matter if none of it was for
us. Just to be in the same dirty room was enough, fingering a
wet book of matches and listening, and looking at them.

After only three days we were all deathly sick already of
each other's faces, voices, shoes, and eating habits. How did
those boys off on three-year voyages in the days of sail keep
from murdering each other? They had no food, no heat, no
comic books, no Bob Hope telling them funny ones over the

radio. Iron men with iron heads. Here we were with our puny little flood and a barge sunk and we were kicking and feeling sorry for ourselves and squawking because cook had lemon instead of blueberry pie for supper. Now if we had been dismasted and laid on our beam ends for three weeks in the Indian Ocean trying to trim cargo below decks in the dark with our bare hands while the other watch manned the pumps we'd have had some right to whine about the way destiny was shoving us around.

I went into the engine room and talked to the Grease Cup and he said we would be laid up three or four hours. I was off watch so I went up and put on my hip boots and waded across the railroad tracks, walking carefully and feeling for the rails so I wouldn't trip and fall down and I slipped around some buildings and got to the street. There was pumps going and water pouring out of buildings, and sandbags piled up around the foundations. There was groups of men in boots and raincoats standing in the rain with flashlights, all giving advice and enjoying the excitement.

I went up to a tavern and sat down on a bar stool and talked to some jerk who claimed the flood was all the fault of the U.S. Government for putting in the nine-foot channel and the locks and dams.

"There is a swell example of them Democrats for you," he said.

"Well there wasn't no traffic up in here before they put in the locks," I said. "There wasn't enough water up here in summertime to float a ten-foot skiff."

"It is just like this here socialize medicine," he says. "They will be operating on everybody and hauling out their appendix all the time whether they want it out or not. And they call this a free country. I'll guarantee one damn thing they ain't going to haul me up to no hospital and lay me out on the table and stick no knives in me because I ain't going to stand still for it. Maybe you want some government doctor sawing off your god-damn leg just because somebody in Washington has got him on a quota, but Joe Pierce ain't gonna *be* there. Joe Pierce gonna be in Canada or someplace. Joe Pierce ain't taking *that* off nobody, lease of all the U.S. Engineers or the War Department. Take this here tax on cigarettes . . ."

"You take it," I says. "I don't want it. I want another beer right now."

"I should think you boys down here on the river would get wise to yourselves. What we ought to do is blow up these locks and dams and end this here flood menace. You boys must like these god-damn floods or you'd get together and do something about it. If it was me why I'd . . ."

"Them dams have been in for twelve years and we didn't have no floods. There is just too damn much water coming down from Minnesota," I said, drinking another beer.

"That's just what I mean," he says, but I saw he was nuts by this time, so I let him rave on while I drank three more beers, keeping my eye on my watch so I wouldn't miss the boat, and it got past 11 P.M. so I left and went out into the street and it was still pouring down in buckets.

I walked down toward the river and I didn't care any more about my troubles and I thought, Well Casey is all right he is all fussed over number 36 going down is why he been acting so foolish toward me the last two days; if the sun would come out and we would make a little better time for a couple of days he would be his old self and see my side of the thing.

So when I got down by the river I was passing an old brick warehouse and somebody says, "Son, could I trouble you for a match?" and I see this old boy standing in a doorway out of the rain. He was a crummy-looking bird with a white mustache and white hair and I could see from the

street light on the corner that he needed a haircut. I stepped
into the doorway and gave him a match and he lit up a stogie.
He had a hook nose and a sharp pair of eyes that looked
right into me.

"What boat you off of, son?" he said.

"The *Royal Prince*," I said.

"Never heard of it," he said. "I don't seem to recognize the
names of none of the boats no more."

"It ain't much of a boat," I said. "I ain't surprised you
never heard of it."

"I been away too long," he says. "I been out West to the
silver mines, and down East, and over to Europe and all over
hell and back. Old Hannibal don't seem a bit the same."

"It never did," I said. "There ain't a hell of a lot to it."

"Now don't talk like that," he said. "A hundred years ago
Hannibal was a right pretty little town. Slow, but mighty
pretty."

"I wouldn't know," I said. "I wasn't here a hundred years
ago."

"No you wasn't," he says. "I never seen you before."

He had on a dirty old white linen suit, which I thought
damn queer, and he hauled out a big turnip of a watch and
looked at it and says, "Getting on toward midnight. You better be getting back to the steamboat, son. The other pilot
will be looking for relief."

"I ain't no pilot," I says. "I am the Mate."

"What you doing uptown while the boat is tied up then?"
he says. "I reckon you wouldn't Mate for me very long."

"Times have changed, old man," I says.

"Yes," he says. "I reckon they have."

"Good night," I says. "You better get in out of the rain."

"After a while," he says. "Good night, Mister Mate."

I took off down the street and crossed to the other corner
and looked back, but he was gone. I went down to the river

and waded across the railroad tracks and went aboard to the
boat just in time to get a cup of coffee and go on watch.

Whatever the engineers had been doing they weren't
finished until nearly 5 A.M. and I went up to the pilothouse
to wake up Ironhat. But he was sitting there in the dark
smoking another one of his cheap cigars, looking at Hannibal
and the river—what you could see of them.

"All right, let's go," he said.

So I went out with the Swede and we turned loose and
started on up the Mississippi and then I went back up to the
pilothouse.

Ironhat blew for the Wabash Railroad bridge above town.

"Did you go uptown?" he said.

"Yeah, I got wet inside and out."

"How was it uptown?"

"The same as it always is uptown," I says. "We are better
off, all of us, down on the river. There is nothing but trouble
uptown."

"I ain't so sure of that," he says. "For example would you
like to run this bridge for me?"

"Not by a damn sight," I says. "If I wanted to run bridges
in the high water with seven barges I'd be a pilot.

"But I ain't," I says.

Now you take Bryan. I lay his downfall to Gum.

—WILL ROGERS

14

CASEY got me on the frying pan the next morning up in the pilothouse and of course he was in such a nice mood he decided to give me the business with friend Jackoniski slumped in a corner taking it all in and enjoying the scene better than a Technicolor movie featuring seminude showgirls stranded on a tropic isle.

"Well I hope you had a lovely time uptown last night," he says.

"Yes," I says, "I did."

"Right in the middle of a flood is a swell time to go chasing all over town for a bottle of whiskey and some tail."

"Yeah," I said. "That's what I thought."

"In my opinion everybody on this here boat has gone nuts," Casey said.

"You won't get no argument out of me on that," I says, looking cool.

"Well I don't want nobody leaving this boat no more. Get that?" Casey says, very tough.

"Yeah," I said. "I got it."

"Jesus Christ, Duke, I thought you had more good sense," says Captain Casey, looking upriver, very stern.

"If I had more sense I wouldn't be here. This ain't no company in which to talk about sense, good or bad."

"Well there's the bank right over there. It don't take no trouble at all to get the yawl out and set you on it. You can go anytime if the company don't suit you."

"I guess I can stand it," I says. "I got a rugged constitution. I can put up with most anything."

Jackoniski spit on the floor and went out.

"That's the kind of a man I like to have aboard," I says. "One who spits on the pilothouse floor." If a deck hand was to spit on the pilothouse floor, or anybody else for that matter, the mighty Casey would have had his heart stuffed and baked for Sunday dinner.

"Well he wasn't uptown in no gin mill last night anyways," says Casey. "He was on the boat where he belonged, by God."

"Why the hell don't you run him for President?" I says. "He would make a good clean-cut candidate."

"What in hell come over you last night anyways?"

"I got sick and tired of listening to the god-damn jabber here on this old beat-up boat, that's what got into me. Since when was it a crime to go uptown when a steamboat was tied to the landing?"

"Since I'm running the boat, that's when," he says. "And don't forget it."

"Seems like I remember when you and I was deck hands

together we use to run uptown quite a bit. Quite a bit we was committing this serious crime of going up two-three blocks for a beer."

"We ain't deck hands no more," he says.

"We sure ain't," I says. "But I wish sometimes *I* was."

"You might get your wish most any time," he says.

"I had enough of this," I says. "If you got anything more to say go ahead and say it. I'm getting a god-damn headache."

"Well while we're at it I might as well tell you I ain't so blame enthusiastic about these here Correspondence Courses and such crap. It don't look good and most likely it will take your mind off your work."

This was sure the cat's ass, coming from Casey. Many is the time sitting around in the pilothouse on the evening watch when he would get me to tell him what I was studying up on and bum some scraps of facts off of me to impress his tavern pals and his dolls with.

"I give up on you," I says. "You must have a bottle hid around here someplace. For a Canadian dime I'd get off at the next lock."

"And leave me in the middle of a flood? Oh no you ain't. You are gonna stay right here. You climb off this outfit and by God I'll guarantee you're through permanent in the Company."

"That's what I like about you big Captains," I says. "You got this notion there is only one Company. This may be a shock to your nervous system, if there is anything left of it, but guess what I discovered? There is *another* company operating steamboats in the United States. Amazin, ain't it?"

"Yeah," he says. "An you are such a big shot you could walk right over and get a first Mate's job in ten minutes, I suppose."

"I got a License," I says. Casey didn't have any more License than a channel cat, and what's more he couldn't get one because he was color blind. He never would have a License and it made him mighty mad, the mere mention of the word. See, you don't have to have License on the diesel boats. Mostly the companies want licensed men because the insurance companies raise hell about it, but if a Pilot was good enough he could hold the job and the company would look the other way. And Casey was good enough. And then some.

"Yeah," he says. "We all know you got License. We hear about it enough."

That was a big lie because I never mentioned the subject one year to the next. I knew I had it and I knew I liked having it better than anything I had and that was enough. I didn't hang it up on the wall of my cabin either. I kept it in my suitcase. Sometimes I would take it out and sit on the edge of my bunk and admire the steel engraving and read it over.

UNITED STATES DEPARTMENT of COMMERCE
Steamboat Inspection Service
License to Mate of Inland Steam Vessels
This is to certify that . . .

"Yes," I says. "I know I am always blabbing about it. Hardly a meal goes by I don't spend the entire time talking about my License. I just don't seem to be able to find nothing else to talk about. Queer, ain't it?"

If you haven't got License it must make a man feel pretty bad at that. Anyway it sure makes you feel good to have it. You have to go to the courthouse, and the steamboat inspectors sit you down and give you about a thousand questions to answer; you have to write them down in little blue books and some of the questions is dandies, what I mean. It is mighty quiet in them examination rooms. Every once in a while the Inspector lets fly at the cuspidor, but aside from that there is nothing much doing. Well you finally get through it in a couple of days and they give you the License, providing you pass. Then you get it framed under glass. And then you are proud, but you pretend it's not much. Except when somebody going up for his License asks you some advice and then you lay it on pretty heavy. "Oh, I got off easy," you say. "I only had 183 questions. Now Slim Harper why he had 235." The candidate turns pale at this and goes back to studying up some more in the books. Or you might say, "Why they really ain't a hell of a lot to it. The written part only took me two days." "Holy Christ, *only* two days," says the prospective licensed mate on Inland Steam Vessels. "And whadda ya mean 'the written part'? Ain't it *all* written?" "Oh my, no," you say. "Why then there's the oral questions. Them Inspectors are allowed to just ask you any damn thing they happen to think of. Anything at all." "Like what for example? What did he ask you?" "Well let's see, now one oral question he asked me was like this: 'If a side-wheel steamer breaks down on one wheel . . .'" "*Side-wheel* steamer? Goddam it there *ain't* no side-wheel steamers. I hardly ever *seen* one, much less answer questions about it. *I* ain't agoing up there and be made a fool of. Side-wheel steamers!" "Well maybe he won't ask you no questions about side-wheelers. Maybe he might ask you something else, like say sparring off, for example. He might . . ." "What the hell is sparring off?" "Why dang it man that's the way they use to get the packet boats off the bar when they would run aground. They . . ." "I ain't never *seen a* packet boat and I ain't never *heard* of sparring off and I be danged if *I'm* agoing up for license after all. It's just plain as can be they are just waiting up there to make a fool of this boy, but *he* ain't going to be there." "Oh it ain't so bad," you say.

"Remember that night we was down in Helena on the *New*

Era?" I said and Casey got down off his chair where he was steering all our big long tow, 800 feet of it ahead of us, up the Mississippi, and went back to the back end of the pilot-house and got himself a paper cup of water. I went up automatically and took the steering bars and held her up for him. It was 11 A.M.—I couldn't sleep again—and the big wide alley was dead under a gray sky that pressed down on everything.

And we were still only just a mile or two above Hannibal; because we had no sooner turned loose the night before and got up through the Wabash Bridge when the engineers called for another shutdown, so we had to tie off again. We could have got the coal moving North just as fast if we'd have all started in with buckets to carry it up the railroad tracks.

"Yeah," he says, sitting down again. "I remember Helena. But that don't change nothing."

"I didn't expect it would change nothing," I said. "But I wonder what ever happened to Thelma and Irene."

"Why bring them up?" he says.

"No reason," I says. "Merely an attempt to bring a little good cheer into the pilothouse."

Casey took off his hat and threw it over on top of the ship-to-shore radio.

"Oh hell," he says. "Duke you are the most miserable man to get mad at."

"I'm a regular caution, ain't I?" I said, sitting down.

"Thelma and that crazy old brother-in-law of hers with the overhalls on. Oh lordy if he wasn't a sketch. And that Irene —her and her cross-eyed sister. My god what a night."

"We missed the boat and tried to get a cab to take us to Memphis, remember?"

"No that was the time we got stranded there when the *Resolute* sank. On Thanksgiving Day."

"I guess you're right," I says. "It was one of them times anyway."

Then we looked at the river for a while. It was a big river and filled with trash and coming down at us mighty quick.

"Duke," Casey says.

"What is it?" says I, wondering what.

"This here trip ain't no picnic for me. They more than raised hell with me over that number 36 going down. You know something?"

"I know a lot of things, but what?"

"We are shoving damn poor and there ain't nowheres near a crest here yet. The crest ain't even passed La Crosse yet. Look over there," he said.

He pointed over to the Missouri side and the water was right up to the railroad ties.

"That ain't nothing to what's coming," he said.

"Oh well," I says. "The mighty *Royal Prince* is making her way. We can't expect no miracles."

"Ironhat is right, although I hate to admit it," he said. "What about?"

"This rig ain't steering right," he said. "She is wanting to run all over. I have to watch her damn close."

"It is just the fast water," I said.

"Well," he said, "she sure don't like this flood. She wants to run away."

"Maybe we got a log jammed in one of the rudders," I said.

"It don't feel like that," he said. "It just feels peculiar somehow. Now it ain't so bad out here in the open river. We got water enough for the god-damn *Lusertania*. But if she don't behave no better we might just naturally collect some drawbridge for a souvenir before long."

"Talk it over with Grease Cup, or with Kennedy," I said. "Maybe they got some clue onto it."

"They tell me Kennedy got to have his stomach cut out," Casey said. He went over and put his hat on again and lighted a cigarette and sat down.

"He's got diesel stomach," I said. "That life down there in the engine room would give me 20,000 ulcers in one short month."

"By the time we make Twin Cities this trip I am going to be ready for three or four operations myself," he said.

"We are shoving O.K., quit worrying."

"Duke, you foolish bastard, do you want to know something?"

"Yes," I says. "I always like to know something."

"We ain't shoving a damn bit good," he says. "And what's more, she is steering like we had left the rudders back at St. Louie."

Do you remember the day I saw you over on
Grandview Ave. that Monday and I said that you
would not write to me when you went back to the
steamboat and I said I wouldn't write till you
wrote but I did and when I put that on there I just
wanted to remind you to write me.

—A DECK HAND'S LETTER FROM HIS GIRL

15

BEFORE lunch I walked out on the tow to look
things over and when I got out near the head of the tow
there was Jackoniski and One Eye and the Kid all peering
down between the barges. A muskrat had got caught in
between the barges and Jackoniski wanted to get him out
and have some fun with him pouring turpentine on him. The
muskrat was crouched down in there on top of the drift,
jammed in between the barges, and Jackoniski was poking
him with a stick. I laid down on my belly on the deck and
reached down and picked him up and carried him across
the deck to the outside of the tow and dumped him in the
river.

Jackoniski went back to the boat.

"He don't seem to care for you too much," says the Kid.

> *. . . it sure meant a lot to me when you give me a date that night I was home instead of Wallie as it give me a chance to get over my bashfullness and to colect something I have been wanting to colect ever since that night I walked you home the first night I ever seen you.*
>
> —YOUNG DECK HAND'S LETTER TO A GIRL

16

AT 1 P.M. the pilothouse radio said the crest was around Winona. The Red Cross was up at Prairie du Chien and half the town was living in warehouses and garages. The Wisconsin was over her banks.

"Oh lovely," Ironhat murmured.

*"I et for two hours and didn't recognize a thing
I et except an olive."*

—TOM MIX AFTER A DINNER
AT THE HOTEL ASTOR

17

THERE was a lot of drift in the river and an old
flatboat floated past us upside down and bound for the sunny
Southland with its skag up in the air. An oil drum was skim-
ming downriver over by shore with a tree right behind it,
and out in the channel there were sticks and branches, an
outhouse, and railroad ties and bridge timbers and boards
and a flight of wooden steps and a butter tub and beer cans
and bottles and a chicken coop, and I don't know what all—
the flood was doing a swell job of house-cleaning.

"Yeah, who was the bright boy said the crest was past?"
Ironhat said, looking at the river with disgust. "Who was the
bright boy made that remark last night? Why look at that

drift. Next thing I expect to see is a whole town coming downriver including the courthouse and the depot."

"I wonder if that there boat is worth going after?" I said. "She don't look so bad from here. I got half a notion to get out the yawl and go after her."

"Don't talk silly. You ain't goin noplace. That would be just fine if we was to bust a coupling or something and you off in the yawl chasing some old sunk john boat. You just set right there where you are. You ain't goin noplace at all off this here tow, not while I'm up here in the pilothouse anyways."

"O.K., O.K., don't blow your stack," I said. "I got no use for the boat even if it is any good. When I get off this old kerosene burner for vacation I got no interest in going for a boat ride for entertainment, I'll guarantee you that."

"If we ever get back to St. Louie from this trip I do believe I'll hang up my cue and call it a game. If this ain't the dangedest way to make a livin I ever heard of," says Ironhat very much put out.

"Well, Ironhat, old boy," I says, "it is a punk trip so far, but anyway we have a nice happy crew. It is nice to see everybody going around with big toothpaste smiles."

Ironhat turned around and treated me to a sour smile.

"The only one left aboard who ain't mad at somebody is the Kid," I says.

"Give him time. He'll probably punch the cook in the face before we see old Eads Bridge again," Ironhat said.

The way Ironhat got his name was that years ago when he was Mate on one of the Barrett Line boats over on the Ohio he went on a two-day tear at Cincinnati and finally showed up down at North Bend with a canary bird in a cage, a broken hand, and a derby hat on. From that time on he was always known, from the Yukon down to the Intercoastal Canal, as Ironhat. I suppose the clerks knew his real name because they had to take his Social Security number and fill out his Group Insurance and all that, but nobody else did.

"If I was Captain on this here rig I would tie her up," Ironhat said. "I'd call that office and I'd say, 'We're tied up. And we gonna *stay* tied up until we get a sensible steamboat river,' that's what I'd say."

"I bet you wouldn't."

"I bet I would. Why don't Casey tell 'em? Why don't we tie up?"

"Did you ever hear of Casey doing anything like that? That's why they gave Casey this trip, so we *won't* tie up."

"You think so?"

"I know so. He'll never tie up, even if the water gets to the tops of the bluffs. I been steamboatin with him for ten years."

Funny thing is, Ironhat would never have tied up either. None of us would have if we'd been Captain, any more than Casey. We was all too dumb and stubborn to do anything reasonable like that.

Meanwhile we crawled on up the river in spite of the best efforts of the flood to shove us back down to St. Louis, and the afternoon wore along somehow under a mournful sort of sky. We seemed to be getting noplace, going through all this for nothing.

And like Casey said, even the boat itself seemed to feel it. That would sound silly to anybody who has not been around boats and listened to them work and breathe, but nevertheless she was sluggish somehow. Working hard, but no heart in it.

"I don't know what's the matter with her this trip, but she just don't feel right somehow," Ironhat would say to Casey when he came to relieve. "By God she's all over the river, and between you and me Casey, even with the flood and all, she ought to shove better than what she's doing."

"She feels all right. She's O.K.," Casey would say. "This

ain't the *Mackenzie*. It's a miracle we're shoving this mess upstream at all. I'd say we're doing a real fine job."

"She don't answer like she ought to, Casey," Ironhat would reply, pausing to make his last entry in the log as Casey sat down in the pilot's chair. "I have to fight her all the way."

"You been listening to too many of them radio-serial programs," Casey would say. "Two days and we'll be above the flood and really start to move."

"I hope so, but I ain't expectin it. The radio says they have three hundred men building dikes way up at East Dubuque. We ain't going to be there in no two days."

The tow looked funny after we lost number 36. There was two barges side by side, then two more ahead of them, then two more, and then one, spiked out there all by herself. It gave the fleet a lopsided appearance and it looked all wrong with that barge stuck out ahead; nobody in our company every heard of a seven-barge coal tow on the Upper Mississippi. Nobody ever wanted to hear of one, either. The whole thing was awkward, no mistake.

The afternoon got more and more mournful and the soap operas coming in over the radio with everybody going crazy didn't help much to add a note of cheer. First it would get too hot in the pilothouse and Ironhat would slide a window open and then it would be too cold.

Presently it began to drizzle again.

"I don't like the looks of things a dang bit," Ironhat said. "But that's your ——in Upper Mississippi for you—either a flood or low water. One trip up last Auust we was aground six times. We was aground at Victory Bend, Richmond Island, Red Wing, below Dresbach—there ain't hardly anyplace we wasn't aground. Now look at her—you couldn't find bottom with a church steeple."

The fact of the matter is, Ironhat was quite a ragged pilot and knew it. He hadn't any too much nerve and without that you are in no shape to be a pilot. When things get tight there is no time to hem and haw and think of various pros and cons of the situation, bawl orders, bawl other orders just the opposite, waste time cussing the company, back her when you know you should be driving but haven't got the guts for it, while your tow gets in worse and worse shape all the time. That is no time to do these things, but in a good jam Ironhat usually did them, glaring at the river with his bloodshot eyes, and always at the last minute realizing what he had to do and squeaking out somehow by finally doing it, just as the whole works was about to pile up on a bridge pier or take out a cluster of pilings.

"The fools," he said. "The blame fools."

The fools was the company, the company who had sent us upriver on a flood stage with a big low-water tow of barges.

"She's shovin about as hard as my old grandmaw and she ain't steerin worth a goddam either," he said. "We could of took four loads and made some money, but that wouldn't suit. No, we had to take every barge in Alton and get right out here in the middle of the highest water since old Mark Twain was a squirt."

He reached up and blew two shorts on the whistle for a deck hand and after a while Arkansaw showed up.

"What's goin on?" Ironhat said as Arkansaw closed the door and stood there in the back of the pilothouse with his cap in his hands.

"Why we're soogin down the cook's room. We are gettin ready to paint it. Just now we are asettin in the messroom drinkin our 3 o'clock coffee. We was just sayin it looks about time to start double-trippin. That's what it looks like to us. We ain't hardly goin upstream at all. Ain't y'all gonna double-trip, Ironhat?"

"Go get me two cups of coffee," Ironhat said. "Make it black and make it hot."

"Yes *sir*, yes *sir*," Arkansaw said.

"Seems to me you been up here long enough now so's you could talk English like a human being. You hate them black boys so, how come you-all talk like they-all? I can't hardly understand that lingo of yours noways. What's the big god-damn idea of it anyways?" Ironhat said.

"I don't talk no different from nobody else down home," Arkansaw says, but the way he said it he sounded like he's on some hillbilly radio program about to saw a few jokes off the corncob.

"Well, go get the coffee," Ironhat said. "And come back sometime before the high water goes down and we run aground."

Arkansaw went away.

"You know how many miles we made in the last three hours?" Ironhat said.

"You tell me," I says.

"How many you think?" he says.

"Oh," I says, "we sure ain't burning up the track none, but, well, we must be making better than two mile an hour. We must of made seven, eight miles."

"Duke, we covered less than four and a half miles. We are making less than a mile and a half an hour."

"That ain't good," I said. "Well, I spose we'll be double-tripping by tonight."

"Yeah," he says. "Casey will sure want to double-trip."

"I hope we can find some grandpappy-size trees to tie off to."

"Unh," says Ironhat.

Double-tripping means that we had got too many barges to shove all at once so we would break the tow in two. We would tie off three barges and leave a watchman on them and then go on up the river with the other four. After we had got up a ways and through some bridges or fast places why we would tie off our four and go back down and get the others and take them up past the other barges where they were tied off until we got up a ways and then tie off *those* and go back after the *others*. If the water stayed mean why we would most likely have to double-trip the whole remaining five hundred miles to St. Paul.

Arkansaw came back after a while with Ironhat's two cups of coffee.

"Ain't we gonna double-trip, Ironhat?" he says. "We shore ain't gettin noplace this away."

"Go long, white boy," Ironhat says, imitating Arkansaw as best he could. "I-all will let you-all know when the time comes." He pronounced "time" kind of like "taa-a-m," a pretty good imitation.

So Arkansaw departed and left Ironhat and me all by ourselves to bore each other to death with complaints and tedious comments.

But we were in for a little unusual diversion that afternoon, at that.

"Hey, what the hell is that over there on the island? Gimme them field glasses," Ironhat said.

"Whereabouts?" I said, getting the glasses out of the case.

"Right over yonder," he said. "I'll be a mud cat if that don't look like somebody on the roof wavin at us."

I handed him the glasses and then I saw where he was looking, over across the river. There was a clearing with a house and a barn and a chicken house and a net reel, most of it half under water, and sure enough it did look like somebody was trying to flag us down. They wouldn't have been up there on the roof waving a rag just to celebrate.

"By God, it looks like a girl," he said.

"That's a damn unhealthy place for a girl," I said. "What's she doing?"

"What the hell you think she's doin, crochet work? She's wavin at us. We gotta get her outa there."

He reached over and hauled the indicators down to Half Ahead.

"Get the yawl out and take a ride," Ironhat said. "I'll hold up out here in the channel."

"Christ, what next?" I said as I went out the pilothouse door.

Zero and the Swede were in the deckroom cutting cards for a penny a cut, so I got them on their feet and in about ten minutes we had the yawl in the river.

Ironhat came out on the bridge and hollered down to me.

"Duke," he says, "take a blanket along. Whoever it is, looks like they are about half nekkid."

I sent Zero after a blanket and then I thought by God anybody over there on a roof half nekkid must also be about half dead, so I went in the galley and grabbed the coffeepot and a mug and set them in the yawl. By that time Zero was back with the blanket, so I started up the outboard. She started up on the fourth lick and away we went, me and the Swede, over toward the island, dodging the drift as best we could. Well we got over to the shore and had to go mighty easy. To get to the house we had to go plumb over the island and thread our way right through the trees, and by and by we came right up to the house.

It was a girl and all she had on was a pair of blue jeans, she didn't have on nothing above that. Swede and I was so surprised we never said nothing at all at first. So we came alongside.

"Come on," I says. "Hurry up now. Here, I'll grab you." And I stood up while the Swede held the boat.

"The hell you will," she says. "I can still get into a boat by myself."

"Listen, no time to argue. Come on. We gotta get out of here."

She was covering up her tits with her arms and she wouldn't come, so I had an idea and tossed the blanket up on the roof. "Here," I says. "Wrap up in that. Now come on. Hurry up."

She wrapped up in the blanket and then she came over and I hoisted her down and set her on the middle seat and Swede turned loose and we got out of there in a hurry.

She had black hair all tangled up and black eyes that really crackled.

After we got out in the river I tapped her on the shoulder.

"How long you been up there?" I hollered above the noise of the outboard.

"Get your god-damn hands off me," she says, giving me a look like I was a rattlesnake she had just met out in the woods.

The Swede was embarrassed and just looked ahead towards the boat. Women made the Swede nervous. The only ones he felt easy with were the St. Paul whores, he liked them well enough.

Over in the middle of the river Ironhat was out on the bridge, looking at us through the glasses. By the engine room all the engineers were standing on deck watching us. Back aft, there was old Clarence in his white clothes, and the mess-boy, and Zero, and they were all lined up gawping and pointing, some big deal.

I had the old outboard pretty well throttled down on account of all the drift and stuff. I wanted to get some coffee into this kid, but I was afraid to nudge her again for fear she would bite off a finger which I might need later on. So I hollered at her.

"Hey, wildcat—here's some coffee," I says.

She turned around and I handed her the cup first and

then passed her the coffeepot. She sloshed out a cup and drunk it down. I had a chance to get a good look at her. Right at the present time she couldn't of passed no Hollywood screen test, but underneath the tangled-up hair and the mud on her face and a cut on her forehead there was a pretty lively-looking kid here. I was wondering right off what she would look like after a little soap and water and a combing up.

"Look out, that coffee's hot," I said.

"No it ain't," she said, and poured out another cup.

"How long you been up there on that roof?"

Now picking a girl off an island in the Mississippi you would expect her to have a couple front teeth missing, or if nothing missing then a general run-down appearance to the dental display, but boys, this girl had those nice whities that you see pictured weekly in your favorite storybooks.

"I been there since yesterday noon."

"You live there?" I said.

"What the hell do you care?" she said.

I laughed. That made her madder. She looked pretty good even when she was mad. Only she looked like the hot independent type that might just get mad enough to pick up an ax.

Anyway we got back to the boat and came alongside and the Swede tossed the bow line to Zero and we flopped in.

I got out and reached a hand down to her.

"Come on," I says. "Hurry up."

"I ain't gettin aboard no steamboat," she says. "Put me ashore someplace."

"Ashore? Are you nuts? Get out, come on."

"My Daddy he told me to never go near them steamboats. I ain't gonna."

"Well your Daddy ain't here right now so you better get the hell out of that old yawl," I says.

"No he ain't here," she says. "But I wisht he was," and by God she begun to look like she was about to blubber. Oh Christ, I thought, if this ain't one sweet proposition.

"Listen, Miss, we'll put you ashore right up the line at Hannibal or Quincy. We can't just dump you over on the railroad grade in the shape you're in."

The Swede and Zero they were standing there wishing they were someplace else, so then Clarence came down the deck.

"You better get aboard, Miss," he said, "I got a hot meal for you and I bet you're ready for some grub, ain't you? I got hot biscuits and ham and black-eyed peas and some lemon pie . . ."

"Ain't nobody gonna hurt you," I says. "*Please* get aboard."

By this time the kid was bawling, she was scared silly.

Ironhat came out on the bridge and saw what was going on.

"Get that yawl aboard," he hollers down. "Get that yawl aboard! We ain't got a week to spend here. Done wasted twenty minutes already. Come on, Duke, for Christ sake get that ya-wl aboard."

Clarence come over and he finally wheedled the girl into coming aboard the old hell-ship *Royal Prince*. I don't know what she thought we were planning—mass rape like South Chicago, or that we might boil her up with some onions into a mulligan. She scrambled up onto the deck with the blanket wrapped around her and her head sticking out the top and tears running down her face. Right about then I begun to feel pretty sorry for this girl and when old Duke gets in that mood it sometimes is a shame the things that can happen.

Anyway Clarence took her in tow. Where I had flunked out a hundred per cent on gaining her confidence, he was doing fine. So he says, "Come on in the galley and we'll get you warmed up, Miss," and we started up the deck, Clarence in his white pants and shirt and cap, the girl behind him in her blanket, and me behind. Well that fancy procession didn't last long because we hadn't taken four and a quarter steps before girl, blanket and all went down in a heap on the deck. The blanket come off and so there on the deck of our old towboat all of a sudden we have a nice young maiden passed out cold and with nothing on but a pair of blue jeans.

She was built pretty good. She looked nice, lying there. But there was no time to write a poem, so I just picked her up in my arms and carried her into the galley.

"We'll put her in the Extra Room," I said. "Come on, Clarence, hurry up. If she comes to and finds me carrying her around like this she'll have another fit and most likely claw my eyes out. She's got a temper, this one."

We had an extra stateroom on the boat, right next to Clarence's. It was for guests, officers of the company, and other royalty, so we put her in there. Clarence hauled the bed open and I dumped her in there pants and all, or pants and nothing, rather, and pulled the covers up.

"Get some more blankets," I said. "This dame is damn near froze to death." So we put two more blankets on her.

"How long she been up on that roof?" Clarence said.

"Since yesterday, she says. I'm sure glad I didn't spend the night on no roof with no clothes on to speak of. I like to froze solid myself out on the tow last night with a good flannel shirt on. Listen, Clarence, ain't you got a hot-water bottle? We gotta steam this dame up."

"Yeah, I'll get it," he says. "She'll be mighty lucky if she don't get the pneumonia." He went away and I fussed around, turned on the steam line, tried the water faucets. The girl was looking mighty pale.

Pretty soon she came to, but she was too played out to set up a squawk.

"What happened?" she says.

"You conked out. How you feel now?"

"When you gonna put me ashore?" she says.

"Up the river a ways. Don't worry about that. The Cook is gettin you a hot-water bottle and something to eat. You just lay there and take it easy."

"Get me a shirt to wear. I lost mine in the river wavin it at a boat yesterday—all the good it done."

"I'll get a shirt. You get warm. You stay there."

"I ain't goin noplace half naked," she says.

I went out and run into Casey.

"Did she come to yet?" he said.

"Yeah, she come around. She ain't spittin quite so hard neither. Ask me, she's about half dead."

"What's she look like?"

"Like a half-drowned muskrat right now. Scrape some of the mud off and I think there's a dame underneath."

"Good looker? How old?"

"Black hair. And half her teeth ain't gone either. Hell, she's only a kid. Can't be much more'n sixteen."

"*Sixteen?* Jesus, we better get rid of her. Them island girls they'd rather do it than eat. That's bad, on a boat."

"I might be wrong, but this kid don't look like it to me."

"Ah, you're always romancin. Listen, how'd she get up on that roof? Where the hell is her folks at? What's her name?"

"Goddam it go on in and ask her, it ain't my job to interview dames. I'm just the Mate, remember?"

"Listen, you picked her up, you and Clarence can just take over. She's used to you by now. We all keep traipsin in there one after another she ain't gonna like it."

"Well she don't like me a bit to start with."

"Ain't that too bad? What'd you do, try and love her up a little?"

"Listen, Casey, get your head up out of the sewer. This kid's half dead. Say, you got any whiskey aboard?"

"Wanna have a party now, hey? I'll tell you what, I'll call St. Louis and have 'em send up a preacher and drop him onto us from a helicopter. Then you can marry the dame and re-tire."

"Christ, you're a scream. You got any whiskey, Casey? That girl oughtta have a couple shots."

"Ask Clarence. I bet he's got a pint someplace," Casey says, walking off up the deck unconcerned. "And tell your girl friend she ain't on here for no excursion ride to St. Paul. Got enough troubles without pussy aboard. She's gettin *off*."

Clarence showed up with the hot-water bottle, looking foolish.

"Go on in, give it to her," I says. "I'm gonna get her a shirt."

"She sure ain't dressed up for no party," he said.

"Say, Clarence, you got any whiskey? Damn, seems like a couple shots would do her a world of good," I said.

He had some rum and he went to fix her some rum in hot tea. I came back with a clean T shirt and a blue work shirt that had CENTRAL BARGE LINES embroidered on the back in yellow letters and gave them to her.

"Well go on, beat it," she says. "Get the hell out. What're you waitin for, the second show?"

"Aw, I seen you already," I said. "Go on, put them shirts on."

"Well, you didn't see much," she says, pulling the T shirt over her head. I'll say she had a cute pair.

"Yeah, that's right," I says. "You ain't got much to show."

"Well don't strain your god-damn eyes then," she says.

About that time Clarence came in with the tea.

"Here," he says. "Drink this down."

"I don't want no tea," she says. She scrooched down in under all the covers with just her head out and all that black hair of hers all over the pillow. Well, Clarence prevailed on her to drink it and she sat up and drank; she coughed and her eyes watered.

"Some tea!" she says. "What'd you put in it, turpentine?"

"That had rum in it," Clarence says. "That's good for you."

"Ain't there no women on this boat?" she said.

"Only you, Miss. How you feel now? You warm?"

"Yeah," she says. "I guess."

"After a while I'll bring you something to eat," Clarence says. "You just lay still, don't worry about nothing," and he went out.

"So long," I says. "You're O.K."

"Yeah, I'm in a hell of a fine shape," she says. "The farm is under six feet of water, Maw and Paw and Frank are all drownded, the cattle and the hogs is all washed off down-river, and I'm laying here in a steamboat. Sure, I'm O.K."

"Listen," I says. "I gotta go. It's not right me alone in here with you. We got a lot of wise apples on this here boat that just love to talk."

"Whadda you care, ain't you the Captain? You got a fancy cap."

"No I ain't the Captain, or anything like it. I'm the Mate. Now, you got any more questions?"

"Yeah. Where's a comb at?"

"Here," I said, and I pulled mine out of my hip pocket and tossed it to her.

"Thanks," she says.

"No trouble. You can keep it," I said. "I'll see you later," and I went out and closed the door.

"Hey!" she yelled after me.

I opened the door again.

"Now what?"

"Maybe you better lock me in," she says. "I wouldn't trust no river-boat man ten feet."

"How about me?" I says.

"I don't trust you neither," she says.

So I locked her in and went out to the galley. Clarence was stirring up some soup, and the messboy was up to his neck in dishwater as usual.

"You ast me there's somethin funny about it, kind of a mystery like," says the messboy clashing the ironstone china plates together in the suds and dropping a cup to the floor with a crash. "Now you take where is her folks at for one thing. I bet she was left up there on purpose. Dang peeculiar if you ast me. How do we know she wasn't kidnaped?"

"How is she?" Clarence said to me.

"Here," I said, and I gave him the key. "This was her idea."

"She ain't so dumb," he said.

"You ast me, she might be a spy . . ." says the messboy.

"Yeah," I said. "There is quite a few young girl spies around these days. You have to keep your eyes open all right."

Dear Mary Lane:

Could you suggest a way whereby I could guide my son to higher ideals without his knowledge?

—LETTER TO THE OMAHA, NEBR.,
World-Herald

18

WE hadn't hardly got anyplace at all by supper-time, so when he went on watch at 6 P.M. Captain Casey decided after he looked at our log for the afternoon that we would start to double-trip, and he begun to look for a good place to tie off the three front loads of the tow. Then he called me up to chew over which deck hand we should leave behind on the barges as watchman.

"I wouldn't blame the boys a bit if none of them would agree to stay on them loads," I said. "Mighty chilly and lonesome, and there's no dry ground within two miles of here. Hell, suppose we run into trouble and don't get back for two-three days?"

"How's the dame gettin along?" Casey said.

"I just looked in a while ago," I said. "She's asleep. She sounds O.K., she ain't wheezing or anything."

"We better put her off at the lock, I expect," he said. "What do you think?"

"I think after what she's been through we better let her sleep. Rest is what that girl needs."

"All right, all right, we'll leave her alone then. But remember, she's your lookout, not mine. I got nothing to do with it. I got other stuff to handle. We'll put her ashore up at Keokuk tomorrow."

"Now you're using your head," I said. "Well, now we got the dame problem settled, who we gonna leave behind on the barges? I wouldn't blame the boys if they *all* refused."

"*I* wouldn't stay on them barges neither," Casey said. "But I ain't a deck hand. If I *was* a deck hand I'd goddam well *have* to. I stood barge watchman plenty times. Near froze and starved to death over near Golconda on the Ohio one time on three empty gas barges."

So we picked on One Eye. He kicked and growled and said he wasn't staying on no tied-off barges in no flood. Said there wasn't nothing he could do there anyways if the barges wanted to bust loose; there was nothing one man could do, and as far as anybody stealing coal why anybody that wanted to come ahunking around in a flatboat on a river with that much water in it to steal some coal why they was more than welcome to it so far as he was concerned. He said he wasn't going to *do* it and that was final; we could put him over on the bank right now with his suitcase.

I told him not to be such a stubborn old fool, he could make out just fine, lay around easy and have a fine old time while we were working. I told him we would leave the big tarp and three or four blankets and kindling and he could burn coal out of the barges and be mighty snug.

"Yeah, mighty snug," he says. "Especially when the whole works busts loose and goes down the river with me aboard."

So I told him we would leave him a pound of coffee and a pot and a loaf of bread and a ring of baloney and a cut of salami and four cans of beans and some bacon and some eggs and a can of peaches and some comic books and cigarettes.

"How many comic books?" he says.

"Whadda ya mean how many?" says Casey.

"All the ones we can round up," I says. "Clarence has a whole pile he ain't let out yet. He ain't even looked 'em over himself yet. I'll get 'em for you."

"O.K.," says One Eye. "But youse better be back by tomorrow."

So he decided he would stay on the barges in the middle of the flood *with* comic books but not without, which demonstrates that the comic is mightier than the sword.

We found some good big cottonwood trees on a drowned island someplace way down below Quincy, Illinois, and we tied off the front three loads. There wasn't any way in the world for One Eye to get ashore; he had the channel on one side and a half a mile of flooded islands and sloughs on the other.

"There's *one* barge watchman ain't going to slip ashore and hike uptown to the tavern while we are gone," Casey said. "He ain't going to get off that island because this time the island ain't really there at all. He won't get thirsty anyways. There is enough water on top that island tonight to run the Cincinnati waterworks for two months."

Kennedy came into the pilothouse while Jackoniski and his deck hands were out with the yawl running lines around those big cottonwood trees and Casey was waiting on them to get finished.

"When do you suppose we are likely to get to St. Paul?"

he said. "I got a date back in St. Louis that I don't aim to break."

"Mr. Kennedy I would sure like to be able to answer your question," Casey said. "But the fact is, I can't even tell you when we are going to get to Quincy and that is only four miles away."

"I got a date in St. Louis," Kennedy said.

"That is between you and the Grease Cup," Casey said.

"When do you *think* we are agoing to be in St. Paul?" Kennedy said.

Casey turned to me.

"Mister Mate," he says, "when do you *think* we are going to reach the beautiful, scenic, historic city of St. Paul, Minnesota?"

"I don't *think* we are going to get there at all," I says.

"Now you see, Mr. Kennedy, our Very First Mate here says we ain't going to get there at all," Casey says. "He don't have no confidence. He's one of these here pessimists. He says we ain't *never* going to come around the bend into St. Paul. Now, what do you think of that?"

"I don't think nothing of nothing," Kennedy says and he went out mad.

One Eye was carrying the tarp and some blankets and kerosene lanterns and stuff out onto the barges he was going to watch.

"He ain't got no life jacket on, I see," Casey said, watching him walk out between the barges down in front of us.

"Jesus, Casey, if I told him once per watch about the life jacket I told him a hunnerd times. He's one old-time deck hand. I just can't keep a life jacket on him more than ten minutes," I said.

I shoved open the pilothouse window and hollered down, "*Hey, One Eye!*" and he stopped in his tracks and turned, all smothered under canvas and blankets and stuff, and looked up at the pilothouse. *"Life jacket,"* I hollered and he nodded his head as well as he could burdened down as he was, and then turned away and resumed trudging out to pitch camp. He already had his library out there, a whole Carnation Milk carton of comics, that was the first load he took out.

We broke the coupling ahead of number 3 and 4 loads and backed out into the stream and then came ahead and began to shove upstream with our four. Over by the island One Eye had set down on the barge coaming and was reading a comic before he even lit a fire or rigged up his tarp. I went out on the bridge and hollered across the water at him: *"Life jacket."* He gave me a cheerful wave and kept on studying his comic with that one good eye.

She shoved a sight better with four instead of seven and pretty soon we come up to viewing distance of Quincy lock.

"Kennedy wants to know when we are going to get to St. Paul," Casey said to the Grease Cup, who came in and sat down in the squeaky wicker chair beside the ship-to-shore phone.

"I hope you told him," the Grease Cup said.

"Duke says we ain't never going to get there," Casey said.

"We'll get there some day," the Cup said, shoving his company cap back on his head and stretching his legs out. His tan drill pants had been washed so much they were turning pale, and almost white in places. "We'll get there, but Kennedy won't be here if he's gonna keep that date."

"How are we shoving with the four?" I said.

"A hell of a lot better," Casey said.

"We ain't just flying up the track yet," the Grease Cup said.

"How long can they keep those locks in operation, I wonder?" Casey said.

"Don't ask me. Call the U.S. Army. Call the Engineers,"

the Grease Cup said. "I bet they can take a lot of water though."

"They can't only take so much," Casey said. "When the water gets to the machinery why they are done."

"That ain't going to be so long neither, if you ask me," I said.

"My God but you are sure in one sweet cheerful mood," Casey said.

"We ain't none of us cutting in on Bob Hope when it comes to that," I says. "I ain't heard nothing to make me split my sides open since I left Katz's drugstore in a taxicab last week."

Casey blew for Quincy lock and after a while we saw the lockmen fooling around and pretty soon the lower gate began to open. When it was open they gave us a blast and Casey took her on in.

"I wonder how your girl friend is getting along?" Casey said.

"Now, Captain," I said. "Keep your mind on your work. You turned her over to me to worry about."

By now it was dark.

That doesn't mean much to look at it. That is like when you read in a book and it says, "That night Higgins froze to death, so we left him on the glacier and proceeded after a breakfast of one biscuit apiece and one ounce of chocolate." You don't feel cold when you read it and you don't feel how it was with the flood all around us when it got dark, just because I am saying it got dark.

We crept into the lock. It looked very cheery with all the lights going strong down both sides and the lock tenders dressed very neat and tidy and waiting for midnight, so they could get in their cars and go home and fry an egg before bed. Up above the lock it was black, and the sky began to leak again, favoring us with a light drizzle.

"You better get some sleep, Duke," Casey said, making his entry in the log.

"I ain't about to sleep," I said. "You might need me before long who knows. I'll just set here and if I get sleepy I'll lay down on the bench."

Jackoniski came up for the locking ticket.

"They got some dumb bastard up there on the lock wall says the locks above Keokuk are closed down," he said.

"I'm going up to the lock house and telephone the god-damn office," Casey said and he went out slamming the door without even putting on his hat.

"I suppose that was your idea," Jackoniski says, lighting a cigarette and throwing the match on the floor although there was sixteen ashtrays around, "leaving my only deck hand on them barges down-river. This here Kid and Stevie between the two of them wouldn't make one half a deck hand."

"Talk to Casey about it," I says. "Or better still pack your other pair of dirty socks and climb up the wall and call a cab."

"That would make you too happy," he says, and he spit on the floor. "Besides, we got a dame aboard now. A young one. I like that young stuff," so he spit on the floor again and went out.

I turned on the radio and somebody won a refrigerator for guessing who Woodrow Wilson was and I turned it off again and wondered what the orders would be from St. Louis. The drizzle was striking the panes of glass on the west side of the pilothouse. I have been in floods before and they never bothered me a particle. In the Illinois River flood in 1942 I was Second Mate of the *Eclipse* and every boat was tied up but us; we were doing sandbagging around the Caterpillar plant at Peoria and general relief work and it was all a big gay party. Everybody said we were heroes. The newspaper reporters interviewed us and put our pictures in the Chicago papers and we had a big time. But we weren't having no big time with *this* flood. For one thing I never knew there was so much water in the world and more coming where it came from. There weren't any reporters or cameramen, just the flood and us. And I wondered how One Eye was making out back there on the other barges. He was probably setting under the tarp reading comics to a kerosene lantern, so I didn't worry much about him.

After a while Casey came back up and he was looking cheerful for a change.

"Well," I says, "did you talk to them? Who did you get? What did they say?"

"I got Hamilton," he said. "He wants us to try to make Keokuk. Canton Lock is still working. We drop two loads at Western Metals and Electric in Keokuk and tie up with the five and wait the flood out. Hell, all the other tows are tied up tight. The old *Royal Prince* is the only boat still working. We will have to hump to get through Canton tomorrow, though, by God. All the water in the world is on the way down—they are going to pull the machinery up there tomorrow afternoon and close down."

"Good," I said. "With luck we will be all tied up tomorrow night as snug as a bug's ear. Now I guess I will lay down until midnight."

"Old Hamilton, by God, Duke," Casey says, "he was positively *friendly*. 'You boys are doing fine,' he says. 'Keep up the good work. There ain't another barge moving between St. Louie and Twin Cities,' he says. 'Is there much water up there?' he says. 'Oh hell, no,' I says. 'Why don't you let us run on up the line? We ain't seen any water yet,' I says. 'I got to hand it to you, Casey,' he says. 'Yeah, but what about number 36?' I says. 'Leave the insurance company worry about that,' he says. 'Call me when you get to Keokuk. And call me in the morning on the radio how you are coming,' he says. 'We are double-tripping,' I says. 'I hope we get to Canton Lock before they close down.' 'Have the Lockmaster there at Quincy call them at Canton to wait on you,' he says. 'I will,' I says, 'but they ain't going to wait when the water begins to come in the front door.' 'Good luck,' he says. 'Luck ain't got much to do with it,' I says. 'Call me tomorrow,' he says and he hung up."

"I never was so very enthusiastic about old Keokuk, Iowa," I said, "but she is going to look like New York City, Denver, and Palm Beach all rolled into one this trip."

"I wonder if Hilda is still around that town," Casey said, the only sensible thing he had said in five days. "If she is, by God, me and old Hilda is going to tie one on that will have everybody hiding under the porches."

"Why, Captain," I says, "you wouldn't leave the boat when she was tied up in a flood and go two-three blocks uptown would you? I'm surprised the way you talk."

"Old Hamilton, Duke," Casey says, "why he was actually *friendly*."

"Maybe he's in love with you," I said, and I went down on deck. I unlocked the girl's door and stuck my head in. She was asleep. She still seemed to be breathing all right. So I went up and flopped on my bunk with my clothes on for a couple hours of sleep.

They'd have lawed me if I had, but I ought to
have shot him and checked the breed.

—ANDY ADAMS
The Log of a Cowboy

19

THE way I got my first job on the river was a fine
introduction to the profession. I was in a joint down at this
same Quincy, Illinois, one time and the Mate off a dirty old
cinder-throwing stern-wheeler come in looking for a deck
hand. I hadn't anything better to do and only sixty-five cents
left in my pants and I was going to sleep under some newspapers in a boxcar that night, so I stepped up and took the
job.

When I got down to the boat and had my beans and
coffee I figured it was time to go to bed, but that was not
exactly the Mate's idea. Ten minutes later I was out on the
head of the barges with the Mate and another deck hand,

waiting for the pilot to give us a toot on the whistle to turn loose.

"My, friend Danny sure bled plenty," says the deck hand.

"Throw some coal dust onto that there blood," says the Mate. "Otherwise somebody tonight after dark might take and slip in it and have a bad fall."

Then I noticed by the timberheads was a lovely pool of red paint or ketchup, only judging from the conversation it wasn't either one.

"How come that blood?" I says, feeling queer.

"Why, Danny, he got his leg cut off down at the piers this afternoon," says the deck hand. "Oh I told him a million times to watch it, I told him what could happen to a body gettin his foot in the bight of a check line. But, *Oh no,* Danny by God he knew it all. You couldn't tell *him* nothing about deckin on a steamboat. You heard me didn't you, Slim? You heard me tell him. Many a time I says to him, 'Danny,' I says, 'you watch them check lines, they will just snatch a leg off, so easy, like *this!*' "—and he demonstrated.

"Where is the leg at?" I said.

"It fell into the river," the Mate said.

"Where the hell is Danny at?" I said.

"Up at the undertaker's gettin pumped full of antifreeze," says the Mate.

"He won't need no antifreeze, Danny won't, not where he's goin," says the deck hand, grinning very cheerfully, and way back on the boat which seemed a mile away to me, the pilot blew a toot on the steam whistle and my career on the Mississippi and other rivers had begun.

When I went to bed after we got the good news at Quincy Lock it was around nine o'clock and I was pretty beat, so I got some sleep. Nevertheless it didn't seem like more than ten minutes I felt somebody tugging at my blanket and saying, "11:30! Hey, it's 11:30. Hey, wake up, it's 11:30. Are you awake? It's 11:30. Time to get up, Mister Duke."

"Oh hell," I thought. "Here we go again," and then as I reached out to find a cigarette in my shirt pocket I remembered the telephone call and the new orders, and Casey talking about Hilda, and the girl we had picked off the roof who was down in the Extra Room in my T shirt.

"Is that you, Kid?" I said. "Turn on the light, pal. Where are we and what's doin?"

The Kid turned on the light over the wash stand and I got up on one elbow and lit a cigarette.

"Christ close the door," I said. "That damp air ain't no encouragement to leap right out of this sack."

The Kid shut the door and leaned against it.

"We tied up them four barges," he said. "We tied them to some big trees. Now we are going down the river after them other ones, I guess. Golly we sure go fast without no barges in front of us."

"Are we still above Quincy?" I said.

"What's that mean?" he said.

"That town in Illinois, did we pass it again yet?"

"No," he said. "We just left the barges only a few minutes ago."

"How would you like to be setting in the sixth row at the Rialto back down in Alton tonight, Kid?" I said. "With a nice big bag of popcorn."

"I wisht you would quit always askin me them questions about how would I like to be back in Alton," he says. "Dang it I *like* it right here on this boat. My buddy over on the *Wheelock Whitney* he was right—there sure ain't nothing to beat it. I figure to stay steamboatin from now on. I *like* it."

"You are a dead pigeon, Kid," I said, "if you like steamboatin after the samples you had of it so far, why I imagine I will be workin for *you* some day."

"How long does it take to get to be a Mate?" the Kid said. I hauled myself up and began to put on my shoes.

"Too god-damn long, Kid," I said. "Way too god-damn long. And when you get to be Mate, why then what are you? Ain't nobody uptown gonna give three cheers when you break the news you are a Mate on a river boat. More likely they will look for the exit or hide the teaspoons."

"Kinda romantic," the Kid says. "That's what I like about it out on this boat. It sure beats workin on a coal truck."

"More like the movies, ain't it?" I said.

"Yeah," says the Kid. "That's what I mean. It's more like the movies."

That Kid, he was a bird all right.

I had time to grab a cup of coffee and check up on the patient again—she was still dead to the world—and then we were at the lock.

We locked down through Quincy about quarter past twelve midnight.

"Better hurry up," the lockman hollered at us as they began to dump the water. "They are holding Canton Lock for you but the water's going up fast. You better be there by noon."

"We'll be there by God," Ironhat hollered back. "You tell them keep that lock open. We'll be there if we have to run a line out and cordelle this whole outfit up there."

I went into the engine room. Kennedy was down between the engines with the Junior Engineer, handling the engines. It was hot and smelly and pleasant in there. That was one thing about the life of an engineer—no matter how cold or wet or miserable in any one of a hundred ways it was out on deck, it was always cheerful and cozy in the engine room. You might say it was too damn cozy down between the engines handling for a couple hours on a hot summer day in St. Louis, but, then, you can't have everything. Even the guys who get to marry Rita Hayworth can't seem to stay satisfied.

After we got out of the lock Kennedy climbed up the iron ladder and went over to the water cooler and made himself an Arm and Hammer highball.

"Looks like you and your stummick are gonna keep that date after all," I said.

"Looks like it, don't it?" he said.

"I hope we get to Canton Lock by noon," I said.

"If we don't, we don't," he said. "Then we tie up below the lock. Who cares? Not me. I don't give a —— where we tie up just so we tie her up. Once we tie her up she can set there three ——in years and it won't bother me none."

"I hope we get to Keokuk," I said.

"Just so we tie up," he said. "The sooner the better. It don't matter where."

I went in the galley and Arkansaw was washing up the dishes from everybody's midnight lunch.

"I wonder if we'll make it," he said.

"I wonder when you washed your hands last," I said. "I believe the only time they ever see soap and water is when you wash them midnight dishes."

"I bet we will lay there at that Keokuk two weeks if we lay there a day," he said. "Will we go on day watch, Duke?"

"We ain't there yet," I said. "And anyway none of them old girls in Keokuk will be able to understand you anyway, so just cool down, boy, cool down."

"I bet there's some old girls in that town that understands two dollars even if they cain't understand me," he said.

I dumped the midnight coffeepot and set up a new pot to cook up.

"Maybe you're right," I said.

"I know I'm right," he said.

The Kid came into the galley and grabbed an apple,

pulled out a big cheap toad stabber he had with a bathing beauty art study on the handle and began to peel it.

"How many movie houses they got in this town where they claim we're gonna stop?" he said.

"Now never mind them movie houses," I said. "We're gonna have plenty work to do. We'll get this old boat all cleaned up and do the spring painting."

"When we gonna get there?" he said.

"God knows," I said.

"Well, I don't care," says the Kid. "I just wondered."

"Tomorrow night we should be all over our troubles, boys," I said. "We'll tie her up, by God, and wait. The water can go clear over the hilltops, we got plenty line to hang on with."

"Ve makin good time," the Swede said.

"Why not, we're goin downstream empty," said Arkansaw. "When we pick up them loads why we'll be shovin again. We ain't gettin noplace. We'll see that there Keokuk, or whatever you call it, about New Year's Day at this rate."

"Why don't they put that dame off the boat?" says Mr. Kennedy, coming in and sitting down.

"That's bad luck, havin a wooman aboard," Arkansaw said. "You look at the record you'll find most always when a boat gets into some trouble or another why there was a wooman aboard. Same with a white horse. In them old times, why no steamboat Captain would dream of takin a white horse on board. Every blame time they did why the boilers blowed up or something. That's right in your history books. That's what my Uncle Fletcher told me, too. He seen it happen more'n once."

"Don't you never run out of them crazy ideas of yours?" Kennedy said. "The reason them steamboats used to blow up all the time in them old days was because half the engineers didn't know a slide valve from a wheelbarrow."

"Ve don't have no vite horse on board ven old steamer

Kate Gardner blowed up. She yust go boom!" says the Swede.

"Say," says the Kid, "what in the heck was they *wantin* a horse on board for in the first place? That don't make no sense."

"Why them was *packets*, boy," Arkansaw said, "they carried everything under the sun. They wan't no trains in them days. You bought a horse in Arkansaw and you wanted him in St. Louis, you either ride him there or ship him on a steamboat."

"Unless he was a *white* horse," says Kennedy. "Then he could fly to St. Louis. All white horses in them days could fly."

"And on these here towboats nowadays," says Arkansaw, ignoring Mr. Kennedy, "why a woman means the same plain old hard luck. Nothin would surprise me." And he took the salt shaker and began to sprinkle salt in the galley doorsill.

"What the hell you doin, man, you gone crazy?" Kennedy said, stirring a glass of baking soda.

"That'll help some to keep the hard luck off," says Arkansaw.

"Yeah," I said. "And it'll help to increase the hard luck if Clarence finds you throwing salt all over the joint."

"Well, anyway, they can't get that dame off'n here too quick to suit me," he said.

Jackoniski came in and threw his gloves on the table-cloth.

"Casey figures to leave her lay until Keokuk," I said. "He's got enough on his mind already."

"How she gettin along?" the Swede said.

"Yeah," says Jackoniski. "How is she? Did you get any yet, Duke, or you just been readin poetry to her? When you gonna let the rest of us in on it?"

"Some day," I said, "somebody is gonna spoil all those pretty white teeth of yours."

"That might be," he said, "but it'll take a mighty good man to do it."

"I got one in mind," I said, "who could handle the job real nice."

"Aw cut it out you guys," Arkansaw said. "Cut it out. Ain't we all friends?"

"Yeah, buddies," I said. "Fifteen happy lovebirds in a cage."

"If you wasn't so selfish you'd let the rest of us at that dame, too," says Jackoniski. "You must be about tuckered out by now anyways."

"Where was you born, in a garbage can?" I said.

"Any time you change your mind," he says, "I got my three bucks," and he sneered and showed his teeth some more. "Give her one, you keep two. A nice profit."

"You talk dirty. Ain't nice," says the Swede.

"Any objections?" says Jackoniski.

"It stinks in here," I said and I went out on deck. I went up on the forward deck to see if the rigging was laid out ready to pick up the other load. Jackoniski had done a half-ass job as usual, so I worked there in the dark for a while getting things straightened out; coiled down the lashings and the locklines and unscrambled some ratchets and wires and got things into a shape where I could lay my hand on something when I wanted it. So I worked and got over being mad, some, although it was an effort. The boat was spinning downstream on the flood like she was just as anxious as the rest of us to make that pickup and get going again upriver, and a chance to tie up tomorrow.

When I went up to the pilothouse Ironhat was also feeling very gay and loaded with good humor.

"*We'll* never make it up there in time," he said. "Another typical example. We could lay up at Quincy, but oh no, we got to do it the hard way, we got to get to Keokuk. If they would take all the combined brains in the St. Louis office and lay them end to end they wouldn't reach across the sidewalk."

"Ironhat," I says, "you are never happy. Why don't you get real thrilled we are going to lay up tomorrow or whenever we get to Keokuk, Iowa, instead of bitching and moaning about it? For my part I am mighty surprised they haven't got some scheme for us where we portage around the locks after they close down. It would be just typical."

We got down river and Ironhat threw the old Carlisle and Finch arc light over onto the loads we had left tied up, and there they were all by themselves against cottonwood trees.

"I don't see no One Eye," I said.

"Now who's moaning?" he said. "He's around there some-place. Probably wrapped up and went to sleep."

We went on down past and made a slow turn and came up to the loads, and I went down on deck to face up to the tow. Ironhat turned on the deck lights and landed against the loads. Zero and Arkansaw got the face wires on, and all of One Eye's gear was there, but no One Eye and I had a feeling right then, even before I went out and combed the barges over, that he was gone to the place where good deck hands go. I took my flashlight and went out onto the barges.

Ironhat had shoved the pilothouse window open and he hollered down in that raspy voice of his, "—— —— —— —— ——."

I went out in the dark night between the barges loaded with coal and I knew he wasn't out there. I looked all around and pulled some hatch covers off and hollered down into the barges, but I knew he wasn't there at all. I went back to the boat and Zero and Arkansaw had finished facing up and had the jockey wires on.

"Where's One Eye at?" Arkansaw said.

"He fell off and drownded," I said and climbed the stairs up to the boiler deck and then on up to the pilothouse.

"One Eye must of fell off," I said. "He's gone. He ain't on them loads."

Ironhat pulled on the overhead light and turned to me with probably the most great combination of amazement and exasperation ever recorded.

"What the hell d'you mean he ain't there?" he said. "He's got to be there. We left him there, didn't we? Where in the hell could he go to?"

"Down for a talk with the fish," I said. "He ain't there because I checked the whole thing over."

"Oh Lord Jesus," Ironhat said.

"You better go get Casey up," I said.

"I ain't going to get him up. *You* go get him up," he said. "But listen, One Eye might of crawled down inside some barge to get out of the rain or something."

"He ain't down in no barge," I said. "Some reason or other he got careless and fell into the river."

I went down and opened the door and went along the corridor and banged on Casey's door a couple times and then went on in. Casey was asleep with the window closed and it smelled very close and sour in there. I flipped on the light.

"Casey," I said. "Wake up. We got troubles." Casey was a very light sleeper and could come out of it in an instant.

"Turn that god-damn light off," he said.

"Wake up," I said.

"I *am* awake. Turn off that god-damn light," he said.

"One Eye is gone," I said.

"Good," he said. "Most useless deck hand I ever seen. Good riddance," he said. "Turn off the light."

"Get up," I said. "One Eye is gone off them loads we tied off. He's gone."

At that Casey dragged out and sat on the edge of his bunk in his undershirt and shorts, looking pale, and freckled on the arms, and with his hair all rumpled up. He reached a cigarette and lit it and dragged one down to his heels.

"Where we at?" he said.

"Faced up to the loads," I said.

"Turn loose and go down-river slow and look for him with the lights," he said. "Hurry up. I'll be up there in a minute."

Zero and Arkansaw cussed and howled about taking all the wires off when they had just spent twenty minutes getting them all tightened up and they said it was a shame the way they was pushed around. They said if One Eye was so dumb as to fall off three loads tied to the bank why it was his own dang fault. They said if he was drownded it served him right.

"We go down looking around in the night for that fool we'll never get upriver in time to make that lock. If he's drownded so he's drownded," Arkansaw said. "Leave him *be* drownded."

"Yeah," said Zero, breaking a twenty-four hour silence. "Leave him lay."

"*Take* them wires off," I said, and kicked the starboard winch loose and pulled the wire back and went out and took it off the timberhead and hung it over the tow knee. Arkansaw done it to the other side. Zero knocked the ratchets loose on the jockey wires.

"Take Her Away!" I hollered up to Ironhat and in the engine room I could hear the bells ring and the boat began to back off from the barges.

"Put them life jackets on now, and keep them on," I said, and I went climbing up through the dark to the pilothouse, feeling the cold damp handrails of the stairs as I went, and wondering what One Eye was doing and where he was doing it—whether he was afloat or on the bottom.

All we needed now for a fourteen-dollar jackpot of nickels spilling out onto the floor would be a nice fog to set down.

This time of year you mostly always have fogs at night when it is so damp out, especially with a flood in progress. But one good thing, we didn't have any fog that famous night.

But it was dark and overcast, and only a purebred pack of St. Louis idiots would be out in the middle of it all, but that's exactly what we were, and *there* we were. I ran my palm over the slick handrails of the steel steps that led up to the pilothouse and I thought of the windows of Katz's drugstore down in St. Louis, all bright and filled with razors and patent medicines and fancy displays of hand creams with the cutout dolls smiling through the Pittsburgh plate glass at you.

"He's disappeared off them loads," I said to Casey and Ironhat as I entered the pilothouse, wiping the wet off my hands onto my pants.

"Then this old girl says to me, 'Well,' she says, 'if you're a married man then that makes it different,' she says," Casey said to Ironhat, who had relinquished the steering to the mighty Captain for the occasion. And he continued:

"I says, 'Now wait a minute, honey, don't be like that,' but she says, 'Oh go peddle your papers,' so I was out about ten dollars for drinks and got nothing out of it at all."

We slid down-river a few miles, supposedly hunting for One Eye, but all we saw was drift and the lights from a freight train over on the Missouri side and all we heard was Casey talking over the girl proposition. He was so happy since he got the orders to tie up and set the flood out when we got to Keokuk that he was not for a minute about to let one sawed-off dead deck hand ruin his good spirits.

"If he had his life jacket on he might of got over onto the Missouri shore," Ironhat said, working the starboard light and shining the beam along the riprap and willows.

"I imagine he's drownded," Casey said. "I don't see nothing, do you Duke?"

"No, I don't see nothing," I said.

"You ain't sufferin no eyestrain," Ironhat said.

"Why that fool," Casey said. "Instead of watching them barges he falls overboard and drownds himself. Now if that ain't a dumb deck hand. Nothing to do but set. But can he do it? No. Things gets so dull on them loads this real brilliant deck hand he gets bored and jumps into the flood. Smart, ain't it? Now anybody want to ask why a deck hand gets them deck hand wages?"

"Well," says Ironhat, "I kind of feel sorry for him at that."

"We went down far enough," Casey said. "Duke, give me the logbook," and I gave it to him. He backed away from the steering bars and Ironhat went back to work.

"Go on back and face up to them loads," Casey said to Ironhat, and he wrote in the log like this, because I read it later:

12:15 A.M. Arrive loads. Watchman Vincent Riley found missing. Conducted extensive search from loads to point two miles south. Search hampered by flood and fog. Returned to loads.

"So one thing it proves," Casey said, "and that is, never tell none of them you are married. It is strickly the wrong move."

"I hope the poor bastard got ashore some way," Ironhat said.

"In the long run," Casey said, "the best policy is not to tell them nothing until you know them real well. After you had a good workout in the sack why they don't care so much you are married. In fact it sometimes seems like it makes them feel mighty gay and proud."

"If we pick up those three and get on up the river," I said, "we'll *still* have time to make it."

"By God we better," Ironhat said.

"But never tell them ahead of time," Casey said. "Tell them after the damage is all over. I never seen a woman yet didn't more or less enjoy it afterwards, to be told you are married."

"*Say, men—*" says the radio which Ironhat had turned on to drown out the captain—"*do you have sandpaper skin?*"

"Well that's the end of One Eye, I guess," I said.

"Get on down on deck will you, Duke," Ironhat said. "Let's pick up these here loads and get on up the river."

It was now 1:30 A.M. in the morning.

It was the mate of the steamer. He gave one look and cried, "O boys—you had better quit."

—CONRAD

20

In the spring of the year the Mississippi River begins to give up its dead. All the newspapers are filled with interesting news items after the ice goes out, referring to various characters who have been missing all winter now turning up as floaters.

". . . was identified by a porcelain inlay," it says. "The body was found by Cletus Willging, wedged between two oil barrels under a boathouse belonging to . . ."

But now it was very spring itself, and if One Eye was ever found at all it would not be next spring. The water was like ice now, but in thirty days it would be warm, and he would be in a punk shape, he would be a poor sight on a spring afternoon when the redwings were warbling in the willows.

In the spring there is always some tired-out corpse showing up uninvited at every river town. They could say a lot of things I suppose, but they say nothing and only serve as a news item and an annoyance, while the ten-cent beers pass across the bar and the kids wonder when the old man is going to come home and give them a smile or a crack on the head.

One Eye would not spend the winter under the pale blue ice in cold storage, for spring was here already, glorious Spring, composed of mud, floods, and the papers filled with new crimes on the outskirts of Detroit. One Eye and a dead hog would get stuck simultaneously in the lock down at Saverton, Missouri, and only one of them would get any attention from a preacher. There would be a little excitement and another one of those UNIDENTIFIED BODY FOUND IN RIVER articles in the local paper.

"I never seen him, but they say he was in bad shape," one of the lock tenders would tell the old lady at suppertime. "They put a door under him to get him out. All decomposted he was."

Casey sat around the pilothouse and we talked it all over, but there wasn't much to do about it anyway and the main worry was whether a fog would shut down and cause us to tie up and miss getting up through Canton Lock. There was mist in the beam of the searchlights and surface fog floating around above the water near the islands and over in the shallow water.

But we made a fast pickup of our tied-off loads and started on up the river, and the fog held off and Casey went back to bed for an hour.

I was on my way up to the pilothouse when I noticed the

light on in the "Extra Room" where the girl was, so I went and knocked on the door. I didn't hear any answer, so I unlocked the door and stuck my head in.

"Hey," I said.

"Hey yourself," says the girl.

So I went in. She was setting up in bed with a whole raft of comic books and magazines. She was reading *Intimate Detective*.

"Say, what's a maniac?" she says. "Do you know?"

"Why sure, we got a few right on board," I says. "Why?"

"Well I'm readin this here story about a sex-crazed maniac. I can't make nothing out of it. What's it mean?"

"Who gave you the books?" I said.

"The other fella. The cook."

"Fine reading for a kid like you."

"I ain't no kid."

"You ain't no grandmaw either. Why the hell don't you go to sleep?"

"I already slept. Then I woke up."

"What's your name, Grandmaw?"

"Marie Chouteau."

"What kind of a name is that?"

"They claim it's French. Don't ask me."

"Listen, Marie, where you going when you get off the boat tomorrow? You got any family?"

"I guess not any more."

"What happened down there at your place before we picked you up?"

"When the flood come we stayed as long as we could. Then we moved onto a piece of high ground. We camped out. Paw and my brother Frank made up a shanty and we was comf'table enough, although we lost the cattle and the hogs. Then day before you come along, why we all went over in the flatboat to see what was goin on and whether the house

was still there you know, and maybe we could save some
more stuff."

"That's bad," I said. "There's an awful current going
through those trees back there."

"Well the current was a good deal more than what we
figured on and first thing you know that old flatboat come
up again a tree and the current got her and dumped her. I
swum over and got on the roof. Maw and Paw and Frank
they drownded, none of 'em could swim a lick. I guess there
ain't nobody left but me now."

"Your folks own that place outright?" I said.

"Why my folks been there close to a hundred years. You
ask anybody down at Springdale if they know Jack Chouteau,
I guess they'll tell you. Why my great-great-grandfather was
related to the St. Louis Chouteaus."

"That don't mean much to me," I said. "Except your folks
owned that place. Well, *you* own it now."

"Gee I never thought of that," she said.

"What you gonna do about it?"

"Who cares?" she said. "It's under nine feet of water right
now. Say, what's *your* name while we're on the subject?"

"Call me Duke," I said.

"Where's *your* folks?"

"I ain't got any more folks than you. Mine burned up while
I was off on the bum one time a good many years ago."

"What did your Paw do?"

"Well he was the champion truss-fitter of North America."

"Now what the hell does that mean? Was there any money
in it?"

"No. It was a poor job. But the old man is dead now,
so we'll leave it go at that. He wanted to do a lot of things,
but he give up too easy."

"He wasn't like you, was he?" she says, wiggling around

in bed with my T shirt on and my work shirt on, of which she had rolled the sleeves up to her shoulders.

"How do you mean?" I said.

"I mean you're a big man on this here boat, ain't you? That wasn't easy gettin where you are."

"Yeah, I'm here all right," I says. "But I ain't planning to stay forever."

"You better stay, Mister," she says. "I bet they pay you mighty good."

"Yeah, they pay me good. But it ain't just exactly paradise bumming up and down this old river. A man wants to settle down someplace, sometime."

"You ain't gonna settle down," she said, reaching for my comb and combing her shiny black hair. Now you wouldn't exactly say this girl was pretty, not in a Hollywood sort of a way, on the other hand you would sure turn around to look at her. I never saw a pair of eyes so black and changeable—one minute they were crackling like fireworks, when she was mad or excited, and the next minute melting like a spring day up the St. Croix River.

"Why not?" I said.

"Ah, you're a roamer," she said. "You'd never stay put no-place after being on these here boats. You got that steamboat fever, like Paw used to say."

"Yeah. I had it. But I'm about over it. You know anything about this 'commercial fishing'?"

"By God I ought to, I been living with it and working at it since I was five years old. Why I can pretty near talk fish language."

"I don't think they got much to say anyway," I said.

"Who?" she says.

"The fish," I said. "They don't lead a very interesting life."

"How long you been an orphan?" she said.

"Orphan?" I said. "I ain't no orphan."

"Sure you are if your folks is both dead, just like me."

"Yeah that's right. I never thought of that," I said.

"It feels funny, don't it?" she says.

"Listen," I says. "I gotta beat it. But listen, Marie, where you going after the hospital, what you figure on doing?"

"What hospital?" she said.

"Why dang it they'll take you to the hospital when we put you ashore, you know, just to look you over—you know."

"You already looked me over," she said, laughing.

"Never mind that stuff now," I said. "What the hell you gonna do?"

"I'll make out. I ain't so dumb."

Yes, I thought, and somebody has got to look after this survivor of the "St. Louis Chouteaus." If she was my girl, I thought, why I wouldn't hardly let her out of my sight. I know these young fellas nowadays, they are just ten times as bad as when I was a kid and we were mighty mean to start with.

"What do you care, anyway?" she said.

"Oh," I says. "I'm interested in your career."

"Yeah, I bet you are. You're interested all right, you don't have to telegraph me that."

"You're cute, you know that?" I said. "You're pretty."

"Aah go away. Why what you talkin about, you gone crazy from ridin this here boat? Now look here," she says—and she holds up a magazine picture of some big movie star—"*she's* really pretty."

"Phooey on her and that china grin of hers," I said. "She got no sex appeal at all. Baby you got three times the stuff she's got. Why you look like you was alive—she just looks like a big mama doll."

"Well then that makes everything real simple," says Marie. "I'll just go to Hollywood and take over her job."

"Well you're a hell of a lot better than her with that baby

stare of hers at least, I ain't kiddin. But I gotta go. See you later, huh?"

"Yeah," she says. "To discuss over my career."

"So long," I said.

"When you puttin me ashore?" she said.

"At Keokuk," I said. "Whenever we get there. So long."

"Well, so long," she said.

So I went out and locked the door behind me and walked up the deck a ways, looking at the river, all dark, and trying to make up my mind. Then I went back and opened her door again and went in.

"Now what?" she said.

"I forgot something," I said.

"What?" she said.

"This," I said—so I kissed her, and then I went out and locked the door again and sort of floated up to the pilothouse.

"Don't it strike you on the cheapness of life, Duke?" Iron-hat said. I had the tow all lined out and the boys standing by ready for the lock which would come up again in a few minutes. "One minute old One Eye is asettin on them loads readin *Horror Comics* magazine and the next minute he is falling into the river and drownding himself like he was some comic-book hero himself."

"I decked with that old One Eye off and on for ten years," I said. "But he's dead now," I said. "The building is burnt to the ground and who seen the mouse?"

"If the fog don't come down on us we'll make it up to Keokuk by tomorrow night," Ironhat said. "And that is the important thing."

"*Say men,*" said the radio, "*do you have denture breath?*"

"Not tonight I ain't," I says. "Come back later for a better answer."

"Casey took it pretty cool on One Eye," Ironhat said. "I figured all the trouble we had he would blow his stack."

"After just so much trouble," I says, "you begin to get use to it."

"But all our troubles are over now, Duke," Ironhat said, and he reached up and pulled the whistle cord for Quincy Lock.

They had the gates open and Ironhat waltzed our three loads right on in and we tied up to lock through.

"Go up and report One Eye to them," Ironhat hollered down to me.

I climbed the wet cold ladder in the lock wall and hunted up the lockman in charge. He had on overalls and a shop cap and wasn't too much interested.

"Report it to Saverton Lock," I says. "He is likely to come up and float in there most any time."

"How come he was on them barges anyways?" says the genial lockman.

"We always leave a watchman when we tie loads off in the brush," I says.

"Don't seem necessary to me," he says.

"Well, they all do it," I says. "It is customary when you leave around two hunnerd thousand dollars worth of equipment and cargo hanging onto an island you also leave a watchman," I says, and went back aboard, leaving him mad.

"The lockman up there, that real bright boy in the overhalls, he don't think it is necessary we left One Eye there in the first place," I said to Ironhat.

"Maybe we should of left *him* there instead of One Eye," Ironhat said. "By the way, how's your girl friend?"

"She ain't my girl friend," I said. "But she's getting along O.K. Experience like that would have killed me, but she's as good as new."

"Say, did I ever tell you about the time I knocked over one

of them pyramid displays of tomato soup in the A & P store?"
Ironhat said.

"That's one I never heard," I said. "But wait a minute.
How is she steering? Feel any better?"

So I left him rattle on although I had heard the tale about
five thousand times, and they opened the upper gate and
we shoved on out into the river and the flood again. Ironhat
told me about the time he was up the Cumberland on the
Princess. And we passed by all the lights, twinkling over
to starboard, of the city of Quincy, Illinois. And we headed
up on the bridges.

"Old Captain Wilson he was a queer duck," says the Ironhat. "Had to have a big bowl of oatmeal for breakfast every
morning. One morning we was coming down from . . ."

We passed under the Quincy Highway Bridge, and by now,
after all the fooling around over One Eye, it had got to be
around 3:30 in the morning.

Ironhat asked me to put new carbons in the port searchlight and it was cold and damp out there, and the lights
on the highway bridge overhead looked dim and misty. I
was thinking that with One Eye gone we would have to
change the watches around some, as the Kid was the only
deck hand left over on the other watch besides Stevie, and
Stevie was nothing to rave about. I figured I would put the
Swede over there, and I would make out with Zero and Arkansaw, but what the hell did it matter anyway—we could
all stand watch steady until we got up there to Paradise,
which was Keokuk, Iowa; it would only be a few hours now.
In our ten-day or ten-week, or three-week layover there, why
in between boozing and going to the movies and loving the
girls I could pick up two dozen deck hands—three dozen:
shag-haired boys with six thumbs, skinny boys with dirty
feet, big strong boys from the corner store with all the latest

tunes, boys named Wilmer with studded belts, and a hundred other boys all dying to go.

"Well, Duke," Ironhat said as he lined her up on the C. B. & Q. railroad drawbridge, "there is the winter harbor right over there, where we could tie off just as easy for the duration of this —— flood, but just so as to see that we don't enjoy life, they have got us headin on up the river."

"Twist her tail, Ironhat," I said. "Twist her tail boy. Once we get through this bridge we'll have a clear track. We can have these here three into Canton Lock by 8 A.M. Then they can come back for the others and be up at Canton easy by 11 A.M."

"I hope so," Ironhat said, lighting a bum cigar and blowing a long blast for the bridge.

Casey was in the sack dreaming of Hilda, the Kid likewise asleep under an itchy blanket; the Grease Cup and the wiper and Clarence the cook, and the messboy were all down inside the steel, asleep. And Marie Chouteau, of the St. Louis Chouteaus. Jackoniski was asleep too, in a special disgusting way probably, with his boots on or dirty ears, sleeping like a hog with an ax in its head.

"Casey never wasted no time over One Eye," Ironhat said.

"There wasn't nothing to do about it," I said.

"Casey sure never paid much attention," he said.

"Ironhat, when you are dead," I said, "nobody pays no attention."

"Go on down and bring up some coffee, Duke," says the pilot. "Two cups, and make it hot."

When I went past the engine room Kennedy was sitting on a beat-up chair by the door on the port side with his chin in his hand, looking out the door where the lights fell on the current sliding past. The Junior Engineer had a wrench and was going someplace to do something; he always either had a wrench in his hand or was going to hunt one up. I stood up on the forward deck and leaned on the big capstan and the bridge tender up the river ahead blew his siren to let Ironhat know the drawbridge was open. The red lights on the center pier were standing bright, and the lights to each side of the draw, too.

"The fog never come down on us after all," I said to the Swede, who was sitting there on a pile of line, smoking.

"Ve be O.K. now, Duke," he said.

"Don't you go lay down noplace now," I said. "You stay right where I can get at you if I need you."

"I stay on deck," he said.

I went back to make the coffee and Chouteau's lights were out again. I turned on all the lights in the galley and thought about the girl as I measured out the coffee and ate some leftover pie.

I went over and leaned out the galley door and we were passing through the drawbridge. Up above in the gloom was the usual dim bridge tender's house with a forty-watt bulb burning behind a window not washed since 1873. The bridge tender was standing on the railroad tracks looking at us disgusted, like all bridge tenders.

Kennedy came down the guard and I stepped back and let him in the galley door. He went over to the glass rack and got a clean glass, took off his glasses and polished them up real fine with a clean bandanna.

"How's your stummick?" I said.

"Same old thing," he said, and put on his glasses and went back to the engine room to wait for 6 A.M. and the Grease Cup to relieve him.

Arkansaw came and peeked in the door.

"Well, One Eye is gone," he said. "You see what I tole you about havin a wooman aboard," and he went away.

I went and got two clean coffee mugs and went over to see what the coffee was doing, when I heard the whistle blow.

One short toot, meaning Mate Come Up to the Pilothouse Right Now.

I thought for a second I could pour the coffee and take it along and not have to make another trip down later. Probably the searchlight was out of adjustment again, or Ironhat wanted a match. But then I thought with the high water and all, who knows, maybe one of the barges had broke loose or he wanted the tow tightened up or something or other had gone wrong, so I set the coffeepot on the back of the stove and went for the pilothouse.

As I went past the engine room Kennedy came out the door like he was shot out of a roman candle and went for the stern.

"The —— steering went out," he said.

Well we are all in fine shape, I thought, as I skinned up the iron stairs hell bent, and I cast a look around. The tow had took off for the Illinois side all cockeyed. We were already in a bad way. The tow had swung over and the flood was beginning to catch the barges and was going to drive the whole works down onto the bridge piers.

When I got to the pilothouse Ironhat was standing there hauling the indicator down for an overload to try to drive her out of it, but the current had got us now. All that water from up North was shoving onto us broadside, and there was no use to think of any way to pull off some miracle of navigation because we were all done and all our swell plans for tonight, tomorrow night, and every other night, were knocked higher than an April kite.

"She ain't coming out of it, Duke," Ironhat said. "She ain't coming out of it."

He threw his starboard light over onto the bridge pier and the water going past it looked like the flood movies in the newsreels. The barges were swinging down, slow, slow, but getting faster as the flood got square onto them.

"Knock the tow loose, knock the tow loose," Ironhat said. "Knock the tow loose. Knock the tow loose . . ."

I flew down to the deck and the Swede was standing there by the starboard winch.

"Knock her loose," I hollered. "Knock her loose. Knock the bitch loose."

He kicked the winch loose and Arkansaw appeared from noplace and went out and pulled the wires off.

"Ve hit, ve hit, Duke," the Swede said.

"Grab a god-damn life jacket," I hollered. Boy I was really screaming by now, and I knocked my winch loose on port side, but I knew it was too late to save the mighty *Royal Prince*. We were broadside to the current now, and the bridge was coming up at us fast.

I ran over to see how far away from the pier we were and the big limestone blocks rose up maybe thirty or forty feet away.

Ironhat blew the emergency blast on the whistle, but he was too god-damn excited, he never pulled the general emergency cord for the inside, for the boys asleep.

I ran over to the other side and ran in the engine-room door. The Junior Engineer was down between the engines handling and I crouched down and hollered at him.

"Get out. Come on. Get out."

But he had the engines on an overload and you couldn't have heard a steam whistle in there that night.

Right then we hit, like the end of the world, and the Junior Engineer fell flat on his tail with a look of surprise. I fell down but I scrambled up and went out the door the down-river side. The boat had already begun to climb the pier and as soon as the flood caught her on the upstream side she would flop over like a shingle.

I scrambled around to the forward deck. Ironhat had the

whistle going overtime. The water began to boil over the
deck and into the engine room.

Ironhat quit blowing the whistle and the water pouring
around us was like Niagara Falls. I ran smack into the Swede.

"I sleep ashore tonight," he said, and he pulled a life ring
down and went slipping and sliding up the deck to the down-
river side. Back aft somebody was screaming bloody murder.

The boat had busted loose from the barges when she hit,
and Arkansaw was out there on the stern end of the tow,
running to and fro in the pale shimmer from the search
lights like a crazy man. The barges hit the next pier over and
were topping around and Arkansaw was the luckiest man
on the Upper Mississippi—those barges wouldn't go down
now, the barges were all right.

The Swede jumped overboard with his life ring and that
was the last ever seen of him, in Quincy or Two Harbors or
anyplace else.

The boat was at a bad angle by now, ready to go down,
down, down any minute, hell, any second. Somehow I got
part way up the forward staircase. I was aiming for the pilothouse, that's that old Mate's instinct for you. But the boat
gave a lurch and I fell down and slammed against the rail
and bounced back down the stairs onto the foredeck again.
The water was coming over the deck good by now, and I
knew our time was nearly up, and I knew what I had yet
to do and I was afraid there wasn't time.

The cabin where the girl was locked in was on the down-
river side, thank God, because all the cabins on the other
side, the port side, were already under water and nobody in
them was ever going to read the Sunday papers again. When
I got there the door was jammed. The boat had racked some
already and jammed the door. The boat give another lurch.

Marie Chouteau was inside, but she wasn't making any
noise. Ten feet away was a fire ax. And so just then the

water got to the generators and the deck lights went out.

"Oh Jesus give me just thirty more seconds," I said. "Thirty more seconds. Thirty more seconds."

Well I knew where that ax was even in the dark and I made a grab for it and got it. And I gave that door a couple strokes I had been saving up. It flew open and I jumped in. She was on the floor. When I blasted the door open it had knocked her down. I dragged her up and shoved her out the door onto the guard.

"Stay there! Don't move!" I said. She didn't say anything. She was too scared.

"Now Jesus give me ten more seconds! Ten more seconds!" I said. On the deck overhead something busted loose with a crash. The bridge tender had turned on his siren now and was filling the whole scene with that mournful wail. "Turn it off, you fathead," I said. "Turn it off damn you and your ——ed up bridge."

I felt around where the life vest should be in its rack, but it wasn't there. Someplace in the boat a low and ornery rumbling began, and the whole boat began to tremble a little. This was it. She gave another lurch. The next one would sure be the last.

Then I felt the life jacket where it had fallen to the floor and slid against the wall. I grabbed it and I was out on deck. I sat Chouteau up and slipped the straps around her. I tied the top strap in a good square knot and right then my ten seconds ran out and the boat wasn't there any more and we were in the water.

The last thing I heard aboard was somebody screaming and then I was in the water going down down down and I was thinking, Oh I hope I clear the wreck and don't get fouled up in something down here. My ears were pounding and I could hear a lot of funny noises—rumbling and bubbling, and things striking together in that dismal hollow way they sound under water. But I was dying for a gulp of air and I began to fight my way up out of it, just hoping to beat hell I would get to the top in time. I came up, and none too soon, either, and the railroad bridge was upstream from me and I was bowling along in the flood headed for the highway bridge below.

Over on the barges in the dark someplace Arkansaw was carrying on in that dialect of his and he seemed so close I could reach out and touch him, nearly, but that was only a trick; voices are mighty deceptive around the water, especially when you are *in* the water and half froze to death.

The boat was gone now, sunk in the flood waters of the Mississippi with God knows how many good boys down there with her. Most of them, I should judge. The whole affair couldn't have taken more than four or five minutes.

"Marie!" I hollered after spitting out a quart of river water. "Marie, where are you?"

"I'm O.K., I'm over here," she hollered back. I couldn't tell where she was, though.

"Swim for the Missouri side," I said. I was busy trying to get my shoes off.

"Marie!" I hollered. "You all right?

"Swim for Missouri, kid! Swim like hell," I said. She must have been in faster water than I was, or else I got turned around. Anyway that was the last I heard of her. She faded away in the flood and the dark.

Well, we are alive, anyway, I thought, and that is more than you can say for most everybody else here tonight.

I hollered at Marie, but there was no answer. I figured she was busy swimming, or else drowned by now. Either one, there was nothing I could do about it.

The water didn't seem so cold, maybe it was the happy thought of being alive that made it feel that way. So I struck out for the Missouri shore; it was heavy going with all my clothes on, but I figured I would make it. I figured I would make it if I had to swim all night. Something had hit me on the head on my exit from the wreck, and I probably would have conked out but for the cold water, so that was a good thing.

Finally I got my shoes off, anyway, and it was a little easier going.

Now I could hear somebody up toward the bridge hollering the same thing over and over, but I couldn't make it out.

Probably the bridge tender cussing us out for denting his bridge, I thought, and it struck me so funny I said it out loud a few times, and then I saw a plank and I tried to reach it, but missed and it went on down past me.

"You might make it and maybe you mightn't, Duke," I said to myself, and I swam some more, a lot more.

Finally I decided to give it up. My arms and legs felt like they were made of cast iron. I was getting sleepy and decided to call it off and get some shut-eye. I didn't care a damn any more, and just then I felt something with my foot and it was bottom.

I crawled out and set down. I was below the Highway Bridge.

"Marie!" I hollered, but she didn't answer.

The siren on the bridge started up again.

"Shut up, damn you," I hollered, "and let a good man sleep."

That was the end of me for then.

Well when I come to I was in the hospital and I had pneumonia and a swell case of it, and was cooped up in an oxygen tent for over a week. They wouldn't give me any news and I had nightmares wondering who got off and who was still down there in that cold water. I was worrying about the Kid. I was having fits over the Grease Cup. I was wondering about Ironhat and how bad he would feel, and whether that Junior Engineer ever took the hint and climbed up out from between the engines and saved his immortal soul for a few more years in the engine room.

I was hovering on the brink for a nice long time and the undertakers were putting in bids, but much to the surprise of everyone I finally come out of it and I asked them to get me a beefsteak and the papers about the wreck.

"I'm sorry," says this little blonde-haired nurse with a snub nose, "but you are too weak. You are not to have any excitement."

"I had enough excitement to kill Bronco Nagurski," I says, "and I lived through it. Get me them papers, honey."

But she wouldn't.

But the doctor did.

And it said the towboat *Royal Prince* had hit the C. B. & Q. Railroad Bridge in a fog, and sunk in the flood, and the only persons that got off alive were one deck hand, and two Mates, the messboy, and a girl passenger. It said the deck hand had pneumonia and was critical.

"What's this deck hand's name?" I asked the doctor.

"That's you," he said. "What *is* your name?"

"I not only got wrecked and damn near drownded," I said. "I got demoted in the bargain."

"What do you mean?" he said.

"I mean I was the Mate on that boat," I said. "But listen, didn't no engineers get off?"

"No," he says. "I don't think so."

"What happened to this girl passenger they talk about here in the paper?"

"She came through it beautifully. Why in three days she was up and out of the hospital."

"She's gone?" I said. "Where to?"

"We wouldn't know anything about that. I suppose she went back to her family."

"She hasn't got any family," I said. "She's an orphan."

"Well, she's gone," he said. "Very plucky girl."

"Yeah, very," I said. "And not bad-looking either."

"Tell me," I says. "What did these Mates look like, and what kind of shape are they in?"

"Oh this one, the good-looking one, he had a broken arm," says the little nurse.

"How do you mean 'good-looking'?" I said. "He didn't have blonde hair, did he? And a big mouthful of pearly white teeth?"

"That's the one," she said. "He had a peculiar sort of a name."

"Jackoniski," I said. "Jackoniski is the name."

"That's it," she said. "He was awfully good about it when we set his arm."

"Jackoniski is good about everything," I said. "But do me a favor, will you, nurse?"

"Why of course. What is it?"

"Put me back in the oxygen tent," I said. "I feel a relapse coming on."

"You've had a bad time," the Doc said, "but you'll be right as rain in a few days."

"Don't talk to me about rain," I said. "And by the way, how is the flood?"

"It is worse than ever," said the Doc.

"Just terrible," nursie said. "Oh the paper this morning showed a picture of some little town just completely surrounded. It was cut off entirely. There was water all around it. It was . . ."

"Sabula," I said. "I'll *bet* Sabula is wet by now. Maybe with good luck the flood will wash that bum town clear away this time." I was mad at Sabula on account of a request made one time for me to leave town and not come back.

"That's not a very nice thing to say," says Miss Bedpan. "Here, take your pills."

"What are these, manhood pills?" I said. "How about you and me going out tonight?"

"Oh!" she said. "And your friend was such a gentleman!" and she went out mad.

"Yes," I said to the walls. "Whatever else he is, Jackoniski is a gentleman, first, last, and always."

Casey was dead. Ironhat was dead. The Kid was dead. Goddam it the Grease Cup he was dead, too. They were all dead except the bums: me and Jackoniski and that fool Arkansaw and the messboy, who didn't even have a name. And the girl, what was she? She was probably a bum, too.

So they turned me loose from the hospital and I went out and got dead, too—dead drunk.

He ain't no bug-eater!

—OLD MAN HUGHES ON THE OHIO

21

AND when I came out of it I went to the window and looked out into the street. It was no street I ever saw before. Or any street I ever care much to see again. Across the woebegotten street was a used-car lot full of cars nobody wanted and next to it a one-chair barber shop with a rubber plant in the window.

The window I was looking through was dirty and the carpet had seen a lot of trouble in its time. I walked over to the bed and there was a real pig there. I don't know much where I picked her up, but there she was. I went in the so-called bathroom and stood under the shower for half an hour and thought of my various errors in life and pretty soon I began to feel better.

So I went in and woke up the pig.

"Listen," I says to her, "what town are we in, sugarplum?"

"Jesus leave me alone," she says rolling over and pushing the covers down, for the poor pig was too warm.

All of a sudden it struck me, where was that suitcase I bought when I came out of the hospital? And the new clothes? But there it was, on a chair, and I went over and looked into it, and my new socks and ties were there. And then I found my pants and my wallet and began to organize for a big departure.

There was six dollars left in the old wallet out of a hundred and ninety bucks, so I must have been having fun, judging from the evidence.

I left the single for the pig to get home on if she had such a place, and trundled myself down through the stinking lobby.

"Well, I'm checkin out," I said to the clerk, who needed a shave, haircut, new shirt, and an education. "How much?"

"You paid up in advance when you and Mrs. Wilson checked in," he said. He needed a new set of teeth too.

"Yeah, that's right," I said. "I forgot."

"Is Mrs. Wilson still upstairs?" he says.

"No," I said. "We had an argument and I cut her up with my clasp knife. I've got her here in the suitcase."

So I went out into the street, where just for the novelty of the thing it was raining some more—raining all over the brick pavement, raining on the bum cars in the used-car lot across the street, raining on an old man who went shuffling by, raining down my neck and onto my good fifty-dollar suitcase.

I checked into an EAT and took over a bowl of Wheaties and some orange juice and bacon and two eggs and three cups of coffee. You sure been making a fine fool of yourself, Duke, I thought, and where the hell do we go from here.

You better get on back to St. Louis and go to the office, get on another towboat, kid, because that's all you know and you haven't got a single place in the world to go to anyway.

"My old lady and me we drove over to look at the flood Sunday afternoon P.M.," says the guy behind the counter. "Jeez the whole town over there is still under water, man that's a sorry sight why they claim it runs into the millions, the flood damage, and I don't doubt it for a minute, why I seen boats goin right up the streets down there on the flats; it makes a person sorry for them poor folks over there, and when I say 'poor folks' that's just what I mean, as usual the rich folks they are setting pretty. *They* don't have no homes down by the river, *they* don't have none of them big *estates* down on the flats you can bet your sweet life on that, oh no, hell they got their big mansions and all up on the bluffs, why that flood water ain't gonna get within a mile of them, but that's the way it goes, like I always say, you can't argue with them hundred dollar bills; you take my boss for example, I don't own this here place, it is owned by Jack T. Weiden-bacher, guess you heard of him before, he also got the John Deere Agency in town and owns half interest in the hotel and is one of the big shots in the Grease Works, well if you think he suffers any you got him all wrong, while I'm asweatin and astrainin here and takin sass off these here high school hot shots that hang out in here why the boss where is he? Why naturally he is over to Toledo Ohio to the K. of C. convention havin a good time, and just bought his old lady a new fur coat a couple months ago—Southern flank muskrat whatever that is—cost him plenty anyways I bet, but that's the way it goes . . ."

"Listen," I said. "Any work around here?"

"Work? What kind of work?"

"Any kind of work. I'm broke," I said.

"You mean you ain't got no money to pay for the grub?"

"No, no. I ain't that broke," I said.

"There ain't no work around here that I heard of," he said. "Unless you want to wash dishes for me until Leo comes back. Leo went to Chicago to have his artificial limb checked over and he ain't got back yet, I suppose he run into some complications with the limb or else got to drinkin again. Leo would be a mighty good man if it wasn't for the drink habit, as I already told him time and again . . ."

"Listen," I said. "How much you payin?"

"Fifty cents an hour," he said.

"Leo must be crazy in the head," I said.

"He ain't too bright at that," he said. "He was over at the saloon havin a short beer when they passed out the brains, haha," he says.

I looked outside and it was raining harder than ever and after I paid for the food I'd have about four dollars left in my pocket, and wandering around in the rain I would get my suitcase all wet. I thought of calling the office for money, but I never liked to let them get anything like that on me. I had nine thousand dollars in the bank in St. Louis, but I had rule about never touching that, not for anything, and I never broke it either.

"Fifty cents an hour, why that's just plain silly," I said. "You can't hire no help nowadays for fifty cents an hour."

"That's right," he says. "But Leo he don't know that. Listen, brother, you brung the subject up, not me."

I went over to the door and looked out into the rain. A driver came in and delivered the potato chips and the cheese popcorn and left.

"I'll work until tonight," I said. "If I get lunch and supper thrown in. And I want a small steak for supper."

"O.K.," he says. "Come on in."

So I went behind the counter and back to the dishwashing department and took off my topcoat and my suit coat

and put on an apron and started in cleaning up the mess.
There was dishes piled up all over the joint but that didn't
faze me a bit, as I have washed enough dishes in my time
so I ought to have a Dishwasher's License from the Department of Commerce, Unlimited Tonnage.

Well there was a lull after the lunch hour and I took the
opportunity to scrub down the kitchen and wash the windows so I could see what was going on out in the alley.
And as I was working away I began to come out of it and a
little bit back to normal. I had to go over the whole thing
again, Grease Cup and Casey and Ironhat and sinking the
boat, and if it could have been avoided, and whose fault was
it, and those things what I should have done that I did not
do, and Milly, the Grease Cup's wife, and Kennedy's stomach ulcers, and the Kid and his old lady back down at Alton, and the rotten noises aboard the boat when she struck,
and when she was sinking, and I thought of Ironhat, spend-
ing eternity in steamboat heaven, smoking a celestial pan-
atela and explaining to the other pilots how he wasn't in the
wrong, going over the whole affair step by step forever and
ever and boring the other pilots half to death, so they begun
to give him the cold shoulder and found some reason to drift
away whenever he came along.

"Well I'll say one thing, you ain't afraid of work," says
the boss. "I don't blieve them winders has been cleaned
since the First Worlds War."

"Leo don't believe in gettin himself overtired, I can see
that," I said. "Maybe his limb bothers him."

So finally I got around to Marie Chouteau and begun to
kick myself around the kitchen about *that*—about her and
her farm down the river, and her and her black hair, and her
sitting up in bed with my shirt on, and her when I kissed her
that time. Oh, I went into the whole thing about her from
top to bottom and from jack staff to monkey rudders and the

more I thought about it and about her the worse I felt, and the view out into the alley didn't lift up the spirits a bit, either.

"Oh, but you are a rotten bum, Duke," I said. "And another thing—you got no sense, no sense at all."

"What did you say?" says the boss, coming into the kitchen.

"Where is the wet mop?" I said.

"Look, you don't hafta mop the floor," he said. "Unless you want to, that is."

"I want to," I said. "Where is the mop?"

"Hangin outside the door," he said. "It's been on vacation out there since last fall, haha!"

So I fetched the mop in and swabbed the floor and entertained myself thinking of all the swell things that might have happened to her such as if she got a job someplace the boss getting fresh with her, wise guys picking her up, her alone adrift in the big city, white slavers—oh I went through the whole book, slamming that old mop around until I got good and mad.

"Why man you're a regular whirlwind," says the boss, sticking his head into the kitchen.

I squeezed out the mop and threw the scrub water into the alley and thought about Marie Chouteau some more, and got so burned up about the whole affair I took off the apron and put on my coat and went out front.

"Hey," I said, "I'm movin on. Pay me off, pal."

"What?" he says. "I thought you was stayin for supper."

"I changed my mind," I said. "I'm goin. I got things to take care of."

"Well you sure done a bang-up job while it lasted. I thought this was too good to be true."

"I put in five hours," I said. "Gimme two fifty and I'll be on my way."

"Oh hell," he said. "You done more work in five hours than Leo done in the last two years. Here," he says and he banged open the cash register and handed me five bucks.

"O.K., I won't argue," I said. "I need it. Say, when can a man get a train out of here to Chicago?"

"Not until 8 P.M. tonight," he said.

"Figure I could pick up a freight?"

"Afternoon fast freight stops here for water in about a half an hour."

"Good. But listen, I still owe you for the breakfast."

"Forget it. Thanks for washing them winders. I never knew whether they was made of glass or what, until today," he said. "Hey, wait a minute, you're about to get hungry on that freight train. I'll give you some sangwidges," and he made up two ham and two American cheese and wrapped them up for me.

"There," he said. "You don't wanna arrive in Chicago on no empty stomach. It's bad enough without that."

"Thanks, buddy, and so long," I said. "Give my regards to Leo."

"Yeah," he says. "But tell me one thing, friend, if I ain't too curious, just what is your regular line of work anyways?"

"Why I'm a steamboat man," I said. "But I got flooded out, wrecked, half drowned, stranded, run aground, and all balled up."

"So that's it," he said. "I knowed you was somethin queer."

"That's it," I said, and I went down and boarded the afternoon freight for Chicago and had a nice fast trip in a Pere Marquette reefer together with two colored boys and a bum named Sam. Sam told me how to get out of the yards and where to go, once we got to Chicago. The rain had stopped and the stars had come out, and I remembered it was spring again although Chicago smelled the same as usual, soft-coal smoke, diesel fumes, and a whiff of the stockyards mixed in.

Sam and I and the two colored boys ate the sangwidges and stood looking out of our boxcar at the lights, and at the broad streets crossing under and over the railroad tracks every which way, at the lift bridges, big warehouses and the back streets with tumbledown little old frame houses. Certainly makes you feel disgusted over the human race when you see the way they have to live, there in Chicago.

"Well bo, where yer wanna go to then?" Sam said. Sam was a lean, scrawny old bum—had been in every jungle in the country, I'll bet.

"I'm goin to Quincy," I said. "But not in no boxcar. You just tell me where that Union Station is, man, I've got my fare."

"Bo, yer showin a very foolish streak to yer nature, there," Sam says. "Why that is downright ree-diculous payin the railroad to ride. Why I can route yer to Quincy in no time, bo."

"I'm ridin the coaches this time, Sam," I said.

"Well if yer so bound and determine, come on, and I'll show yer where to grasp a streetcar," said Sam.

Why that's a regular nightmare—like a horror comic, those railroad yards in Chicago at night. Well we didn't get into the worst of them at that. We hopped off out a ways and I followed Sam, and it was some hike too.

We straggled out onto a street and walked a hell of a ways until we found a tavern and I bought Sam five glasses of wine at fifteen cents a glass and myself a couple of shots so that left me eight dollars and fifty-five cents.

I got down to the station and wandered around and there is one thing nice about the Union Station in Chicago and that is you don't have to live there. An hour in that waiting room with the ceiling three hundred feet high and unhappy soldiers sitting on the benches thinking of home and you want to go out and jump in the conveniently located Chicago

River. There is a good bar there, but if you go into the bar, by the time the train comes you can't raise the price of a ticket. Or you can buy a copy of the *Chicago Daily News* and read the letters to the editor on what is the matter with the Cubs, and Household Hints on how to make cute salads for a bridge luncheon, or doings of the Junior League; however, the best thing to do is get on a train as quick as possible, any train at all.

In this case the train in question was a mule called 7-33 Daily, leaving Chicago at 12:15 A.M. and stopping to rest up at every crossroads on the way to Quincy, including Galva, St. Augustine, Bardolph, La Prairie, Ewbanks, and several dozen others, all in all taking eight hours which I spent smoking cigarettes, looking out the windows at the dark and dismal farmlands, and reading in the timetable about the Free Colorado Springs side trip from Denver to Colorado Springs and return granted to holders of Round Trip Tickets destined Boulder, Fort Collins, Greeley, Longmont, Loveland, Lyons, Grand Lake, et cetera.

Nothing like riding on a train, though. Once I get on a train I don't really care *when* I get where I'm going, providing I get a comfortable plush seat. You cut right through towns and people's back yards, but you don't have to worry about them, you can just close your eyes and let the train rock you to sleep. When you get where you are going you have to get out of the train and start struggling again, but as long as you are inside you can do as you please and watch the sorry world slide past the windows as though you were looking at it through a telescope from Mars.

I got off the train in Quincy at eight in the morning and the train went off to Missouri without me, across the bridge under which the remains of the boat lay sunk with all the boys aboard. And the next thing I did was to leave my suitcase at Nick's tavern and walk down to the river, much as I hated the job. I had to go and have a look at it, so I decided to do that first and get it over with.

The Mississippi had reached a crest and was in full flood. "Run, run, damn you," I said when I saw it. "You drowned all my friends. Why stop now? Why not rise up and flood the whole republic? Get up out of the valley and flood the whole lousy state of Illinois while you're at it. Flood Springfield and Peoria and the crummy old Union Station in Chicago. Wash all the cornfields clear away to Baton Rouge. Go to it, goddam it."

But she just kept on tearing past Quincy, Illinois. Across the river were our coal barges, they hadn't suffered any, just hung up, no doubt, and somebody had tied them off. I walked up to the winter harbor and there was a couple houseboats tied up in there, also some beat-up sand barges and a dredge, a lot of skiffs and floats and an old tugboat. There was one old boy there, one of the houseboaters—he had made quite a haul towing things in out of the flood, timbers, oil barrels, runaway skiffs, and such. He was crouched over the engine in his big flatboat working on it. A big old hound came down the gangplank of the houseboat to look me over. A woman came out and threw a pan of potato peels into the river, looked the river over for a minute, and went back in.

The old boy saw me standing there and he said, "She needs a new water pump. But you know something? I'm just that stubborn that I ain't *about* to lay out eighteen dollars and fifty-five cents for no water pump."

"That's a hell of a lot of money for a water pump," I said.

"Well, that's what you run into nowadays, whether it's water pumps, soap, shotgun shells, or whiskey. Why whiskey alone has got so dear a man can't hardly afford to get drunk no more."

"That's the truth," I said. "Say, is this river at a crest yet?"

"That's what they say. Day or two she ought to start down again," he said.

"Where you come from?" I said.

"'Bout ten miles down-river. Island 435 they call it on the map, some calls it Hurricane Island. It's a good layout. But when the flood come I says to my wife, 'Mae, we're goin up to Quincy for a while, and get in that winter harbor. We're gettin outa here right now.'"

"You know anybody down there named Chouteau? They got a place right on the river. House and barn, he's a fisherman."

"Why hell yes I know Jack Chouteau. That is, I did know him," he says. "Him and his old lady and Frank is gone, drownded in the flood. Marie she got picked up by a steamboat. Picked her right off the roof of the house. She was up there three days and nights, so they say. When they got her she was unconscious. Well then, guess what happened?"

"The boat she was on hit the bridge up yonder and sank," I said. "But the Mate got a life jacket on her and shoved her in the river. So she was saved."

"Yeah," he says. "Say, who are you, anyway?"

"I'm the Mate," I said.

"The hell you are!" he said. "My God, ain't that something now."

"I was luckier than most of them," I said.

"You sure was, boy, you sure was."

"You seen anything of her?" I said. "By the time I got out of the hospital she was gone."

"No, she ain't been here yet," he said.

"I'd like to see her again," I said.

Down by the river in the springtime it smells different than anyplace else. Along with a chilly dampness there is the smell of mud and dead fish and marine engines. And somebody most generally has a boat, up above the high-water

mark, turned upside down, having a new plank put in—and
the smell of the white lead and shavings and paint mixes up
with the smell of trees coming into leaf. Anybody that has
lived around it gets to be mighty fond of it.

"What about that place down there, on the island, that's
hers now, ain't it?"

"Well now, you put it that way I reckon it is her place.
Right now it ain't much of a place though—it's under about
six feet of water."

"Chouteau make any money fishing down there?"

"Told me he cleared over five thousand last year. He fished
scientific. You know, modern. Then, too, he does a little farming. Course he had Frank and Marie to help him. Them two
kids was worth more than all the hired help in the whole
county. Why, my boys I got to work 'em over with a club
just to keep 'em awake. But not them Chouteau kids."

"You mean Marie knows this fishing business?" I said.

"Ought to. Never seen old Jack out runnin nets in my
life, but what she was in the boat too."

"The house any good?"

"Dang tootin she's good. Six rooms, electric refrigerator, all
insulated, copper screens, hardwood floors. Only he oughta
jack her up eight feet and set her on concreek columns."

"How much would that cost?"

"Four hundred dollars. Saaay—what the hell is this? How
come you so interested in Jack Chouteau's landing?"

"Well it's like this, friend," I said. "I'm the one who hauled
Marie off that roof, and after she was on the boat—well, I
got to talking to her about one thing and another. We got
to be more or less friendly."

"Uh huh," he says.

"What do you mean by 'Uh huh'?" I says.

"Nothin. Nothin at all, pardner," he said.

"So I'm naturally curious to know more about that place of hers down there. O.K.?"

"O.K. Sure. Fire away," he says.

"O.K. then," I said. "How many acres to it?"

"Eighty."

"Clear title?"

"How the hell do I know?"

"Probably got a lease. How's the barn?"

"Good. I helped build it."

"What's the water supply?"

"Deep well."

"Make their own juice?"

"No, R.E.A. He run a line in a mile and a half. I helped him."

"Where's his nets and fish gear? Gone in the flood?"

"Up in the hayloft. He moved everything up there. He got over three thousand dollars in nets alone."

"Reckon the barn is still there?"

"It was last week. I took a run down to have a look."

"How's the road in?"

"All weather. Him and Frank dumped gravel whenever they wasn't nothing else to do."

"That's good. They got a telephone line?"

"Why of course."

"Healthy down there?"

"Uncle Ed and Aunt Mary Delefield been livin on the upper end of that island since they was married in 1891. Uncle Ed is eighty-six and thinks nothin of pullin a skiff upstream two-three mile to fish. That sound healthy enough?"

"How far is it to town from Chouteau's place?"

"Oh, six mile to Hannibal by water. Ten mile by the road."

"A man could live pretty cheap down there, I expect."

"Oh hell, off the fat of the land."

"When you goin back down?"

"Soon's the water drops some. Two weeks or so."

"You stayin all summer?"

"Listen, buddy, what's this all about anyway? Sure I'm gonna be down there all summer. I park 'bout half a mile from Chouteau's, right behind a point. Good shade and deep water. But what the hell do you care?"

"I'm gonna need some help," I said, "getting that place going again after this flood. I'll give you a job if you want some extra work."

Well the old boy was surprised, but so was I.

"My name is Partridge," he said, sticking out a greasy mitt. "Charles T. Partridge. But they mostly call me Slim."

"I'm Duke Snyder," I said and we shook hands standing in his old flatboat with the flood around us.

"Come on in the house and have some coffee," he said.

"O.K.," I said. "But I got one more question to ask you."

"What's that?"

"Where's Marie Chouteau?"

Naw, I didn't get any. I had a good time though.
She give me her picture.

—DECK HAND ON RETURN TO BOAT AT ST. LOUIS

22

"How the hell do I know where Marie is, boy?" he said dipping his boots in the river so he wouldn't track mud into the house. "You're so all-fired innerested in her, how come *you* lost track of her?"

"Well, it's like this," I said, as the hound came up and stuck her nose into my hip pocket. "You probably in your lifetime have seen something you wanted, but at the time you said to yourself, 'Oh hell, that's too much trouble' or 'too expensive' or 'Well I'll think it over for a while,' and then by the time you had made up your mind you wanted it real bad, why it was too late by then, and you kicked yourself all around saying, 'What a fool I was to miss out on that, and now

I can't have it, I missed the boat, it's gone.' Ever have that trouble?"

"Oh not moren a few hunnerd times," he says. "Ethel!" he says to the hound. "Keep your dang nose to yourself. What's the matter with you anyways?"

"Aw she's O.K.," I said.

"She don't shine up to very many," he said. "Independent, she is. But what a hunter! Come on, less get some coffee."

This Slim was a lean and bony old boy about forty-five years old with an eagle beak on him and a big mop of hair. He wore a pair of clean overalls that had been patched and patched, a blue flannel shirt, hip boots, and a mashed-up old felt hat.

So we went in the houseboat. Talk about Home Sweet Home, say they really had it made. Linoleum floors, everything neat as a couple of pins, nice new curtains out of the catalog on all the windows, and a smell of coffee and beef stew floating around in general. This was a good-sized houseboat, not one of your decrepit old antique shanty boats; she floated on a hundred and ten steel oil barrels. There was a good big kitchen, living room, two bedrooms, a regular bathroom with a tub, and a shop at one end. Some deal.

Slim's wife had a pie about ready to put in the oven. She had on a cute apron and looked like one of those dames in the Bisquick or Rinso ads, little old typical American housewife ready to buy all the advertised products. She must have been fifteen or twenty years younger than Slim, she looked around thirty or so. Her hair was up in pin curls, she had on some make-up, a nice neat dress and nylons—and here she was living on top of a flood as unconcerned as you please.

"Mae, this here is Duke . . . what did you say your last name was?"

"Snyder," I said.

"He's the Mate off that steamboat that's layin out there sunk in the bridge span."

"You was pretty lucky," she said.

"I was lucky all right," I said.

"You related to the Snyders down at Hannibal?" she said.

"No," I said. "I come from upriver a couple hundred miles."

"I know some lovely people up at Fountain City, Wisconsin," she said. "They own the Palm Gardens Tavern."

"I been in there a plenty of times," I said.

"Well, you sure was lucky," she said.

"How about some coffee?" Slim said. "Take off your coat and set down. Had any breakfast yet?"

"Yeah," I said, lying, because I hadn't.

"Well anyway, give us some of them doughnuts you made yesterday, Mae."

"I will if the boys left any," she said. "The way them boys light into a pan of doughnuts is a sight."

Slim and I sat down at the kitchen table.

"Duke here, he's huntin for Marie Chouteau," Slim said, as she set down the coffee and went to hunt up the doughnuts.

"Man, this is nice here," I said. "Why this is a hell of a lot better than most places up town."

"Well, my God, I should most certainly hope so," Slim said.

"What you lookin up Marie for?" Mae said, setting the plate of doughnuts down.

"Oh, I just want to see her," I said. "Say, them doughnuts look mighty good."

"My last batch was a lot better," she said.

"Go ahead, dive in," Slim said.

"I been expectin her to drop in," Mae said. "If she comes down to have a look at the river and sees us tied up here,

why she'll sure come aboard. And would I be glad to see her!
What she been through, the poor kid. God knows what she'll
do now, without no folks . . ."

"Maybe she ain't coming down to look at the river no
more. Maybe she's seen enough of the river for a good long
while," I said. Out the windows on all sides all you could see
was water; even on the bank side there was water. Out in
the river the current was running past in full flood, greasy
and fast and meaner-looking than ever, with trash and drift
scooting along, or caught in whirlpools and slowly turning
and twisting in circles. And over across by the point there
were eddies and boils on the surface, and the trees were bent
over, some of them pushed over flat and wiggling in the current, and others ready to go any minute.

"Oh a thing like that wouldn't kill the river none for her,"
Mae said. "That kid is just crazy for the river. Just plumb
crazy for it. Fish? My God that girl knows more about fishing than ninety-nine per cent of your commercial fishermen
around here."

"That's what I was tellin him," Slim said, dunking another
doughnut.

"Don't this flood make you kinda nervous?" I says to Slim's
Mrs.

"Not so long as we're up here in this here winter harbor,
it don't," she said. "Anyway, I been through plenty floods before. There is one thing we know for certain sure about a
flood, and that is, it ain't going to stay forever."

"You sure got a nice place here," I said.

"Have some more coffee," Mae said, pouring some.

"How you like it here, I mean this houseboat life?" I said
to Slim.

"Like it? Why dang it man, I like it fine. Why wouldn't I,
I never knew nothing else. Why me and my brothers and
sisters we was *all* born on houseboats."

"*I* was born on a steamboat," says Mae. "My dad he owned a steamboat."

"She's more high-toned than me, you see," Slim said. "Her Daddy owned the littlest steamboat in the history of the world. It was so small they had to hire a midget crew. No regular-size man could get into the engine room. The boiler was made out of a five-gallon lard bucket, and she could raise steam and run full-stroke for twenty-four hours on one hod of coal."

"He's just jealous," Mae said, winking at me and lighting a cigarette. "He's just put out because my folks was big steamboat operators."

"Yeah they sure was," Slim said. "And the handy thing about it was, if the steamboat broke down why they could just load it on a buckboard wagon and take it to town for repairs."

So they kidded each other back and forth for a while and I looked around at the calendar over the stove and the cups hanging on their cup hooks and the double drainboard sink and the spring coming to the valley outside in spite of the flood and I thought, *Damn,* but this boy is smarter than me and Ironhat and Casey and all of us crazy steamboaters with our foolish ways and our wandering habits; a man has got to quit this knocking around forever on these old workhouse steamboats. Oh yes, it is all very glamorous and daring, this carefree life, soldiers of fortune and all that endless crap, and looking out of hotel rooms into the brick streets, and watching the dawn come up over East St. Louis or East Dubuque or East Winona or East Moline, and throwing your money around in the river-town bars to impress the local boys, and bumping down cobblestone streets in taxicabs at 3 A.M. and swimming away from sinking steamboats, and telling big stories in the pilothouse at night while you creep up through Dark Slough or Betsey Slough or Coon Slough in the

moonlight and the pilot unfolds his life history in slow install-
ments night after night—all very romantic no doubt and
worthy material for some snappy up-to-date Jack London-
type master of corn, but the living of it all, that's a different
tale entirely.

"Well anyways—" Slim said, taking off one of his rubber
boots and capsizing it to shake out a piece of gravel—"I suppose you'll be on your way to St. Louis now to get another
boat. This here one up in the drawbridge ain't going noplace
for a while."

"I ain't going noplace at all," I said, "until that girl shows
up."

They didn't say anything to that for a while. Mae got her
darning basket from the other room and came back and sat
down and began to work on a sock. Slim rolled a cigarette
and gave me the makins. Outside Ethel the hound strolled
up the bank and flopped down for a scratch, and a couple
of redwing blackbirds flew by.

"Maybe I'll quit steamboatin," I said. "I don't feel the same
about it lately as I used to."

They let that slide by. Out on the bank Ethel went over
and sniffed a dead fish.

"I been knocking around since I was sixteen years old," I
said. "That can get old, too."

"I made a trip to St. Paul once upon a time," Slim said.
"Deck hand on the old steamer *Morning Star*. Once was
enough for me. It's interesting all right—educational, as they
say—but it was too far from home to suit me."

"I got no home," I said. "So that part of it doesn't bother me
a particle."

"Well, there is only one way to get a home," Mae said, "if
you ain't got one."

"What's that?" I said.

"Why *make* one, that's all," she said.

"Yeah," I said. "They claim it takes two."

" 'It takes a heap o' livin' to make a house a home.' That's quite a thought, ain't it?" Slim said.

"He read that in the paper. He didn't make that up," Mae said.

"I guess if a person was to live *alongside* of the river it would be as good as steamboatin," I said, "and without the inconvenience."

"From Chouteau's landing it's about half a mile to the district schoolhouse," Slim said.

"Schoolhouse?" I said.

"It's closer to a mile, I think," Mae said, rolling up a pair of socks and setting them aside and starting on a blue chambray workshirt with an elbow hole.

I looked out the window at the bank and a couple of inches above the water's edge was a dirty line in the sand, the high-water mark.

"Slim, look!" I said and I got up and went to the window on the shore side. "She's past the crest, she's going down."

They came over and we looked, and sure enough, I was right.

"By God you're right, Duke," Slim said. "Look, Mae, see the high-water mark! She's going down. Old river got tired of botherin the hell out of us and decided to go on down. Goddam!"

"I tole you these here floods don't stay up forever," she said. "Just what I got through tellin you."

So she was through with the idea, the flood was, she had raised all the hell she could think of and sunk the *Royal Prince* and drowned Marie's folks and caused misery enough to go around for everybody, and now she had got over the notion and decided to give it up and let folks have another chance. Now, I thought, the islands will slowly appear again, and the towheads and bars come into sight, and people whose houses have been drowned can soon come back and begin to shovel the mud and brush out of the living room, and the salvage crew from St. Louis will come up the river to raise the *Royal Prince;* they will come upriver with a good clean powerful big towboat and some empty barges, high power pumps, and chains, and the diver crew will swell around on the boat talking about different jobs they have been on, and checking their air pumps or patching their diving dresses. Oh it will all be different from now on, and the rabbits, in a month or so, will be back scampering around on the islands among the sprouting weeds, and the talk will start all over again in the pilothouses of the towboats making their long beautiful trips up the Mississippi to St. Paul. And the engineers will stick their heads out of the engine-room doors again to see what town they are passing, and the deck hands off watch will wander out onto the barges away from the boat to sit and smoke in the early evenings and watch the sun go down over the western bluffs. It will be starting all over again.

"I don't know," I said. "I might go back steamboatin at that."

Way up at the top of the bank a girl was standing looking out over the river. She was kind of a slender girl with a dark coat on but no hat and a breeze from over in Missouri was blowing her hair around.

"Well, that's that," Slim said. "We'll have a little drink to the memory of old friend flood, even if it is only ten in the A.M. Mae, get out that elderberry wine."

"All right," Mae said. "Providing you guarantee not to drink up the whole blame bottle."

"Get it out," he said. "The danged old flood is slackin off. We got her licked, honey," and he grabbed her and gave her a big hug.

"Oh now go way," she said. "You act so darn silly."

"Got a right to act silly," he said. "Now we can get back down-river soon and commence to live again."

That girl up at the top of the levee began to walk down the slope.

Mae got out the elderberry wine and three glasses and we sat down again, all feeling very fine, and watched the sun shining in onto the linoleum floor.

"Well, here's a go," Slim said. "This here wine I picked the elderberries right off the head end of Chouteau's island. Here's a go, and no more floods ontil the next one."

"Yes," I said. "Here's to all of us that lived through it. And here's to the boys laying under water up in the drawbridge that didn't."

Ethel the hound was sitting in the sand scratching her ear, and when she saw that girl coming down the slope she gave up the scratching, floundered to her feet, and ambled to meet her.

"Don't hold back, this here is a big event," Slim said. "How you like that wine?"

Ethel began to wag her tail.

"Better and better," I said.

"Here," Mae said. "Plenty more where this came from. Charles," she said to Slim, "I believe this wine is an improvement over last year's."

The girl picked her way through the trash on the shore over toward the gangplank, with Ethel alongside wagging her tail and licking the girl's hand.

"Sure it is," Slim said. "Things are gettin better all the time, ain't they, Duke?"

"Sure looks like it," I said. "I don't believe I'm going back on the boats after all."

You could hear her footsteps on the gangplank.

"Now who's that I wonder?" Mae said.

Then there were footsteps on the deck and then a knocking on the door and the world stopped dead in its tracks.

"Looks like we got callers," Mae said.

"I'll get it," I said, and I went to the door and opened it up.

She was standing there, and she looked a lot different than when we picked her off that roof one afternoon in the middle of the flood. And a man has got to find a home sometime, and a black-haired girl to take care of him.

"Oh my," she said. "What are you doing here?"

"Waiting for you, Marie," I said. "Just waiting for you."

*But a real woman gets to be more of a pleasure
every year.*

—PEACHES

23

THE Grease Cup was right there in front of Katz's drugstore waiting for us like he said he would be.

"Hello, Grease Cup," I said. "It looks like you got the worst of it again."

"Duke! Damn it am I glad to see you, boy!" he said.

"Yeah, that was bad there for a while," I said. "I thought we had misplaced you for good."

"You wasn't the only one. It was touch and go, Kid. The old man with the bony knuckles pretty near had me that time."

"He got the most of us, at that," I said.

"Ain't you gonna innerduce me to your lady friend?" the Cup said.

"Why dang it, you don't need no introduction—this here is Marie Chouteau, the girl we picked off that roof in the flood."

"Go along," he said. "Is that a fact? Well, you can't blame me. Last time I seen you, Miss, you was a little bit on the bedraggled side. Say, you're lookin swell."

The first thing I did when we got to town was go down to the Boatmen's Savings Bank and draw some money. Then I took Marie out and bought her five hundred dollars' worth of clothes—everything from the inside out, and top to bottom. She had on a cute little hat and a pretty dress and a nice spring topcoat and some dandy new shoes with silver buckles on them and I knew I had made no mistake. There wasn't a prettier, sweeter girl in St. Louis that morning and I knew it. So did the Grease Cup.

"But what you doin now, Miss? You workin in St. Louis?" the Grease Cup said.

"I guess Duke better tell you about that," she said.

"Is that so?" he said. "How do you mean?"

"Let's go get some coffee," I said.

"What's goin on around here," the Grease Cup said. "All right, let's get some coffee."

By now it was late in April, but the sky was filled with scudding clouds again, and whenever one passed in front of the sun all of St. Louis suddenly looked gray and dismal. Then again the sun would come out and it would be warm and Marie's silver buckles would sparkle in the sunshine. Up from the river on the east wind came the sound of a steamboat whistle, a deep one. Blowing for a landing.

"I don't suppose you heard no orders," the Grease Cup said. "Did you call the office?"

"No, I didn't call the office," I said.

We went into a restaurant and sat down at a table.

"Well, what's it gonna do?" the waiter said. "The paper says rain, but it don't look like no rain to me."

"I agree with you," the Cup said. "How's the coffee holdin out?"

"Fine and dandy. Three coffees. Anything else?"

"Bring me a sweet roll, too," says Marie.

"Yes, ma'am," says the waiter and he went away.

"Well Duke," the Grease Cup said, "what's it all about? When we goin up to the office? You know what I heard? I heard the company bought the *Paragon*. Not the old one, the new one. Twenty-two hundred horse opposed piston Fairbanks and Morse. She's a good shover. I bet they got you and me all slated to go."

"I heard that, too," I said.

"You know what I was thinkin? With Casey and Ironhat both gone, they must be hard up for pilots. I bet you can walk right in that office and get the pilot's job on that old *Paragon*."

"That new *Paragon*, you mean," I said.

"You know that channel like the palm of your hand by now, I expect. Duke, I bet you can get that pilot's job."

"I bet I could, too," I said. "But I ain't going to."

"Why not?" says the Grease Cup.

"Here you are, folks," says the waiter, setting down the coffee, and a sweet roll for the girl.

"In the first place even if I was going back I wouldn't want no pilot's job. But I ain't going back."

"That pneumonia must of went to your head," the Grease Cup said. "What do you mean, you ain't goin back? You goin with some other company? You got a better offer someplace else?"

"A much better offer," I said.

"Well, don't keep up the suspense, what is it? What company you goin with?"

"I'm going where all the good steamboat men say they're going but never do. I'm going ashore. I'm taking over Marie's place, up there by the river where we picked her up. I'm gonna fish, I'm gonna farm, I'm gonna sit on the front porch and watch the steamboats go by. And at midnight, when it's time to go on watch again, I'm gonna roll over in bed and give the old lady a kiss and I'm gonna think of you boys sweating it out on the steamboats and I'm gonna laugh and laugh and laugh."

"Aw you ain't gonna do that, Duke," the Grease Cup said. "You're just talkin. You ain't yourself yet. Dang it, who'm I gonna have to shoot the . . . to talk to on the *Paragon* if you ain't aboard?"

"Jackoniski is still around someplace, you can talk to him," I said.

"That's a great idea but he ain't around. He beat up some dame in East St. Louis and got three years in the pen to think it over. Damn near killed her."

"I ain't a bit surprised to hear it," I said.

"Who's that?" says Marie. "Some friend of yours?"

"Yeah, him and Duke was great buddies," the Grease Cup said.

"How do you like St. Louis?" I said to Marie. "You having fun?"

"I want another sweet roll," she said. "I never had one just like it before."

"Oh," says the Grease Cup. "Everything's different down here in St. Louis."

"Tell me what happened to you after that boat hit the bridge pier," I said. "You was missing so long you never even got in on all the publicity."

"Duke, tell me you ain't quittin the river, will you?" the old Grease Cup said.

"Tell me how you happened to turn up alive," I said.

The waiter brought Marie another and fancier sweet roll.

"Well, I got a life vest on just as she was goin down. I couldn't make the shore and I went right through the dam, the rollers was all up of course, wide open she was. So about the time I was ready to freeze to death I got ashore, onto a little piece of high ground way below town. Luck was all that saved me. There was a summer cottage up on stilts there in the trees. The dawn begin to break and I found the cottage. So I busted in, found some matches, lit a fire, found two pounds of coffee and half a case of beans, drank coffee and ate beans for a week until finally a fisherman come by in his boat and I flagged him down. Best time I ever had in my life. Good feather bed—about five years' back issues of *Fur Fish and Game* and *Successful Farming*—a ratty old deck of cards—but I can't hardly look a bean square in the face no more."

"I thought you was dead," I said. "I felt pretty punk about it, George."

"There was even two bottles of whiskey there in that cottage. I lived good, Duke. But I was worried about my wife. I figured havin me reported dead would just about finish poor old Milly off."

"How'd she take it?" I said, although the subject of Milly was one I would usually just as soon stay away from.

"Warm your coffee, gents?" says the waiter, bringing the Silex.

"That's the queerest part of the en-tire blame affair," the Grease Cup said. "Say, boss, how's the pie department, got any good berry pies back there?"

"Why sure, we got blueberry, cherry, and raspberry."

"Raspberry pie? I never had that," Marie said.

"Two raspberry," the Grease Cup said.

"One cherry," I said.

"We got chocolate with whipped cream, too," the waiter said.

"All right," the Cup said. "Bring the little lady a raspberry *and* a chocolate whipped cream."

"I told you this St. Louis was a wild town, honey," I said.

"Yeah this here town is wide open when it comes to them tantalizing pastry goods," the Grease Cup said.

"What were you saying about your wife?" I said. "She still, uh, the same?"

"Why like I said, Duke, that's the queerest part to the whole shootin match. I figured when she heard I was dead she would go crazy the rest of the way, as she already had a damn good start. Well, sir, Duke, it worked out just the other way round. It snapped her plumb out of this trance she been goin around in for the last ten years. Why the old girl she's that changed I hardly know her. She give up them picture shows, she put up new curtains and began to take an interest in her cookin again, she is pallin around with girl friends she ain't seen in years, went uptown and bought herself some new clothes and had a permanent wave put into her hair, and damn it if she don't want to—excuse me, Miss—well she wants to have a baby!"

"Baby!" I said. "But didn't you tell me she couldn't have no . . ."

"That was all in her head. I took her around to the doctor and hell, he said she could have as many kids as Mrs. Dionne."

"Well I hope you space 'em out a little better," I said. "Say, I wondered what you been looking so cheerful about all morning."

"Here's your pie, folks," the waiter said.

So we lit into the pie and drank a couple more quarts of

coffee. Marie would take first a bite of the raspberry, then a bite of the chocolate. The Grease Cup was getting a big charge out of her.

"What do you think of my girl?" I said.

"She's got a good appetite," he said. "That's a good sign."

"I got relations here in St. Louis," she said. "You know any of the Chouteaus?"

"No I don't, Miss," the Grease Cup said. "But if any of 'em look like you I wish I did."

"Nice going, George," I said. "Just for that I'll pay for the grub."

"I guess I better be gettin on up to the office," he said, "before they give that engineer's job on the *Paragon* to Slats Conway or Joe Harper or somebody."

"Wait a minute," I said. "Plenty of time to get up there to that office. You got the seniority and the license, you'll get the job."

I paid for the food and we ambled out into the street. St. Louis was still there, waiting for me.

"Where we goin now?" the Grease Cup said, adjusting his new hat that was still a size too small.

"We're going over to the City Hall," I said. "I'm trading in my Mate's License on a Marriage License. Me and Marie here are gonna get married."

So we all walked over to the City Hall together. The sun had gone under again. Maybe the paper was right about rain, but I didn't care. With Marie Chouteau along beside me it could come down in buckets, the sun could stay under for good if it felt like it, we could make our own sunshine and have some left over.

So you see the high water did some good after all.